CHRISTMAS TO THE RESCUE!

A HEARTSPRINGS VALLEY SWEET ROMANCE
(BOOK 1)

ANNE CHASE

Thomas Publishing

ISBN: 1945320028

ISBN-13: 978-1945320026

For my dear friend Pepper Frost, who loves Christmas even more than I do.

CHAPTER 1

*I*t was the sign in the window display that did it. The Adopt-a-Pet sign with the adorable photo of the cutest, fluffiest dog that Becca Jameson had ever seen, its coat of shaggy white fur begging to be hugged. She paused, captivated by the dog's joyful expression, and felt a tug of warmth and longing.

"Help a pet find a home!" the sign said. "Join us this Saturday at Heartsprings Valley Veterinary Clinic. Our strays need a home for Christmas."

Becca bit her lip, trembling with the realization that she was a stray, too — a newcomer to this small New England town. The dog in the picture looked so friendly and playful, his spirit shining so brightly. So much like she used to be. So much like she wanted to be again.

Could she be that person again? Did she have a chance to find lightness and happiness again? That was exactly why she'd moved here. A fresh start in a new town, a new job as the new librarian of Heartsprings Valley Public Library. Surrounding herself in books, tackling with determination the challenges of a big move and a new job in a new place, moving forward past the heartbreak and loss of the past three years.

Tears threatened at the thought of what she'd left behind. No tears, not now — that would not do! Hastily, she pulled a handkerchief from the pocket of her winter coat and dabbed her eyes. A brisk breeze brushed her cheeks, which were pink with cold despite the brightness of the afternoon winter sun. The warmth of her coat — thick and long and dark blue, with lovely downy lining in the hood keeping her snug and warm despite the crispness of the day — reassured her. Sometimes it was the little things that mattered most.

She needed to be sensible right now, she told herself, even as she felt the tug of that wonderful picture once again. She'd been in town for just three days. Most of her boxes were still packed up. The idea of adopting a dog right now was crazy — pure and simple. She'd barely moved into her cozy little cottage on the outskirts of town. She needed to be practical. No way, no how!

And yet.... As the threat of tears abated, she realized another feeling was stirring within her, this one a familiar and welcome friend. A friend who tempted her way too often. The reason was easy to understand. After all, she was standing in front of the display window of a store dedicated to that delicious friend.

She stared up at the name on the window: Abby's Chocolate Heaven. And inside the window were some of the most mouth-watering chocolates she had ever seen. Rows of gorgeous truffles — dark chocolate, hazelnut, almond, raspberry, lemon, and more. Nougats to die for. Caramels and brittles of all sorts.

Maybe she couldn't adopt a dog today — but she definitely needed some chocolate!

With a determined step, she pushed open the door to the store and was immediately enveloped in the welcoming aroma of cocoa and spices. A heady warmth embraced her. The walls were decorated with all the trimmings of the holiday season — garlands of holly, Christmas ornaments, and ribbons of red and green.

Behind the counter, a woman with a kind face and brown hair, shoulder-length and flecked with gray, gave Becca a warm smile. "Welcome to Abby's Chocolate Heaven," the woman said. "How can I help you?" Beneath the woman's white apron, her red holiday sweater showed a reindeer with a familiar red nose.

"I need a chocolate fix in the worst way!" Becca said gratefully.

"You've come to the right place," the woman said with a laugh. In her early forties, about a decade older than Becca, the woman had a welcoming way about her. Even though she was a complete stranger, it somehow felt to Becca like they had known each other forever. "I'm Abby, by the way."

"So pleased to meet you," Becca said. "I'm —"

"Let me guess. You're our new town librarian."

"That's right. Becca Jameson. How did you know?"

"We've been looking forward to your arrival for several months," Abby said, "ever since Hettie Mae announced her retirement."

Becca thought fondly of the woman who'd hired her to take her place as town librarian. "Hettie Mae is such a treasure."

Abby smiled. "And she is so happy you're here. She is so excited about enjoying her retire-ment — traveling on cruises with her husband and spending time with her grandchildren."

"I'm happy to be here, too," Becca said, real-izing as she said it how much she meant it. "I take it this is your shop?"

"All mine," Abby said proudly, adding with a

laugh, "all three hundred and eight square feet of it."

"It smells so wonderful," Becca said, breathing in the delightful aromas. "And you've done such a lovely job with the Christmas decorations."

"Thank you," Abby said with a twinkle in her eye. "We take our holidays very seriously here in Heartsprings Valley — you'll find that out soon enough!"

Becca's eyes wandered to the rows of exquisite chocolates lined up in the display counter. "I can tell you have such a talent for this," she said, taking in the scrumptious offerings. "They almost look too beautiful to eat."

Abby laughed. "I've always wanted to do this, and when this space opened up on the town square, I knew my chance had arrived."

They got down to the important business of selecting the dozen delicious pieces that Becca decided she simply had to take home with her. Picking which ones was nearly impossible, but Abby helped guide her.

Eventually, Becca picked four truffles (dark chocolate, lemon, raspberry and caramel), four nougats (caramel, dark chocolate, rum, and peanut), two brittles (chocolate mint and milk chocolate), and two caramels (honey and hazelnut).

"Would you like to wrap these up?" Abby said when the red candy box was filled.

Becca smiled, admiring the beauty of the twelve pieces in the box, as her stomach rumbled in anticipation. "No need — these are my treat for me."

"I noticed you looking at the Adopt-a-Pet sign in the window," Abby said. "I'm heading to the vet's clinic to help out after I close up. Why don't you join me?"

"Oh," Becca said, filled with a sudden mixture of hope and anxiety, "I really shouldn't. I'm afraid I'd scoop up every dog and cat there is and take them all home with me before I even knew what I was doing."

Abby laughed. "I'm just like you — when it comes to pets, I have no willpower. If you'd like, I can be the voice of reason, whispering in your ear that you must be strong."

Yes, Becca thought, she must be strong. "Are you sure?"

"Absolutely," Abby said. "I can introduce you to some of the other folks who live here. We're a small town. Everyone will welcome the chance to meet our new librarian."

"Then I'd be happy to join you," Becca said. "Thank you."

"Have you had a chance to acquaint yourself with our town square? It's beautiful at any time of year, but at Christmas it really becomes something special."

"Not really, not yet."

"I tell you what. I have about fifteen minutes of work to do before I close up. Why don't you get acquainted with the square and I'll join you when I'm finished in here?"

"Is there anything I can help you with?"

"Nonsense," Abby said with a smile. "Now shoo. I'll see you outside very soon."

Becca smiled. "See you soon!"

CHAPTER 2

The weather outside was brisk, with a crisp breeze stirring her senses after the homey warmth of Abby's Chocolate Heaven. Becca blinked in the late afternoon sun, adjusting to the bright light. Her breath filled the cold air around her.

Grateful again for the coziness of her heavy winter coat, she took another deep breath and looked around. Abby was so right — the town square was beautiful! Covered in a light dusting of snow, it looked like a postcard of a picture-perfect New England town, brought vividly to life. The four streets surrounding the open square were filled with stores and small businesses of all sorts. She spied a hardware store, a flower shop, a cafe, a bookstore — oh, yet another temptation! — and more. She promised herself that, as soon as she had the time, she was going to explore each and every one of them.

With just two days left before Christmas, it was hardly a surprise that the streets and shops of the square were bustling with townspeople. Families with excited children filled the sidewalks, dodging shoppers loaded with last-minute gifts.

A pang of remorse and guilt hit her. Had she made a mistake moving to Heartsprings Valley so quickly? She'd insisted on arriving here before Christmas, over her mom and dad's objections and despite not knowing a soul besides Hettie Mae.

"You'll be so lonely," her mom had said, "especially at Christmas. You don't know anyone there. Christmas is a time for family."

"I know, Mom," Becca had replied. "But I don't have a choice. The job starts the week before Christmas."

Which was a *lie*. Yes, she'd lied to her own mother! Not her finest moment. But how could she tell her mother, who she loved and honored and trusted so much, that the past two Christmases at home had been the most painful of her life? That the family traditions of the season only magnified her loss of her husband? How could she tell her mom, in a way that didn't hurt her feelings, that breaking free of the past meant starting fresh right away?

She couldn't bring herself to do that. Not when Christmas meant so much to her mom, and her dad, too — he sure did love carving the Christmas turkey! As much as she loved them, she knew she needed to be brave and begin moving forward again. Even if it meant missing her family's annual gathering — with her mom and dad and two brothers and their young families — and spending Christmas in a town where nobody knew her.

Except Hettie Mae, of course. And now Abby. She had a wonderful feeling about the two of them — like they were going to become good friends. Hettie Mae was a true mentor. Oh, the things she knew about libraries and life. As the town's librarian for thirty years, she had a wealth of knowledge and experience that Becca was eager to draw upon.

They'd spent the afternoon together at the library, with Hettie Mae taking her on a tour of the two-story building, showing her every nook and cranny of the rambling structure. The musty, familiar smell of the books had been so reassuring. The joy of reading had always been such an important part of her life. And now she was immersing herself in books — protecting them and promoting the habit of reading for an entire town. A gust of wind hit her then and she shivered — not from the cold, but rather from anticipation of this new chapter in her life.

Hettie Mae's manner tended toward firmness, but Becca knew that underneath lay a generous heart.

"I want you to join me and Frank for Christmas Day dinner," Hettie Mae had told her that afternoon, in a tone that meant that Becca shouldn't even think about arguing. "It won't be anything fancy this year — we'll be too busy packing for our cruise — but we'd love to have you."

"Oh, you don't have to worry about me," Becca had replied.

"Oh, yes I do," Hettie Mae said firmly. "And this is not a request, it's an order! Until I officially retire next week, I'm still your boss." Hettie Mae said this with a no-nonsense stare, squaring her shoulders, looking for all the world like an active grandmother preparing for battle!

Becca had laughed. "You don't fool me, Hettie Mae."

Hettie Mae tried to keep her face stern but couldn't, and she laughed. "Frank and I want you to spend your first Christmas in Heartsprings Valley with someone you know. Right now, that means me. You will come, won't you?"

"Of course," Becca said, grateful for Hettie's concern. "I'd love to be there."

"Good. Now, let me show you the filing system...."

Becca smiled as she remembered the exchange. Yes, her decision to move to Heartsprings Valley had been impulsive, but her heart told her she'd made the right choice.

In the center of the town square, she noticed a large bandstand. Curious, she crossed the street and stepped into the square for a closer look. In the warmer months, she guessed, the square was covered in green grass and flowering plants. But now, with winter swirling around them, the ground was blanketed with a light dusting of snow and the tree branches were bare. The path she walked along was crunchy with salt beneath her winter boots.

And the Christmas decorations! Every tree was swathed in ribbons and lights. The path was lined with beautiful ornaments. Becca could only stare with wonder at the literally dozens of snowmen, snow-women, and snow-children, with their carrot noses and coal eyes and top hats and scarves, who greeted her along the path, alongside reindeer who pranced and frolicked. Abby had said that Heartsprings Valley took its holidays seriously — and she wasn't kidding!

The bandstand was a raised platform with a

half-shell as a backdrop. On the stage, a man with thick white hair and a bushy white beard, dressed in a red winter coat fringed with white, was busy setting up chairs and adjusting a microphone. He looked like Santa Claus himself as he hummed a tune that Becca recognized as "Deck the Hall."

She heard a familiar voice call out "Becca!" and turned to see Abby bustling up the path toward her.

"I see you found the heart of Heartsprings Valley," Abby said.

"It's so amazing here," Becca breathed. "The decorations are so beautiful."

Abby gestured toward the stage. "Every evening at dusk during the Christmas season, carolers gather to sing the songs of the season." She gestured to the Santa Claus lookalike on the stage. "That's Bert Winters, the director of the chorus." At the sound of his name, Bert looked up from his chores. He saw Abby and waved.

Abby waved back. "Bert, I'd like you to meet someone." Bert's gaze moved toward Becca. "This is Becca Jameson, our new librarian."

Bert rushed to the edge of the stage and reached a hand down. "Welcome, young lady, welcome!" Becca reached up to shake Bert's hand. "We've been looking forward to your arrival."

"Thank you, Bert," Becca said, as her hand got

pumped quite vigorously by the enthusiastic man. "It's a pleasure to meet you."

"Bert is Mr. Everything here in Heartsprings Valley," Abby said. "He organizes the carolers, plays Santa Claus at the hardware store, runs the snowplow to clear the streets after big storms, and is the town's mayor."

"You're the mayor?" Becca said.

"Only until I find someone else foolish enough to take on the job," Bert said with a chuckle. "You wouldn't happen to know how to fix a snowplow, would you?"

"Me?" Becca said with a surprised laugh. "Not a chance!"

"Had to ask. You never know. People know the darnedest things."

"Why are you asking?" Abby said.

"The darn thing won't start, and my nephew Billy won't be able to drive up to fix it until the day after Christmas."

Abby said, "But aren't we due for a nor'easter on Christmas Eve?"

Bert nodded. "We might get socked in for a day or two. I'm letting folks know — would appreciate you spreading the word."

"Sure thing," Abby said, then glanced at the setting sun, which was dipping fast toward the horizon. "Becca and I are headed to the vet's, so I'll let everyone there know."

"Thanks, Abby, much appreciated." Bert turned to Becca. "Young lady, welcome to Heartsprings Valley."

"Thank you, Bert," Becca said. "It was a pleasure meeting you."

Abby took Becca by the arm. "Now — it's time for some serious puppy love!"

CHAPTER 3

*A*h, puppies. Perhaps her greatest weakness after chocolate!

"Are you sure about me going with you?" Becca said, somewhat anxiously, as the other woman led her across the square.

"Don't you worry," Abby replied, reading her thoughts. "I promise I'll help you stay strong." She laughed, then added, "At least, I promise that's what I'll do — if that's what you still want me to do after you get there."

"Oh, no. I'm gonna need all the help I can get!"

The vet's office was one block off the main square, in what looked like an old-style, three-story Victorian mansion. A sign in the front said, "Heartsprings Valley Veterinary Services," and underneath that were two names, "Nick Shepherd and Gail Strong, Veterinarians."

Becca looked at the big house, with its shingles and turrets and beautiful bay windows. "This big old house is a vet's clinic?"

"It sure is," Abby said. "It used to be the family home of the Heartsprings clan, the family that founded this town generations ago. The last surviving family member was a dear woman named Minerva Heartsprings. She loved animals — was passionate about their care — and became very fond of Dr. Nick in the last years of her life. When she passed a couple years back, she willed the house to him, on the condition that Dr. Nick dedicate the property to taking care of animals."

"Oh, gosh," Becca said, taking in the strings of holiday lights decorating the building. "That was very generous of her."

"Well, Dr. Nick has done a wonderful job with Minerva's bequest, along with his partner in the practice, Dr. Gail. Even with the heartache and sadness of the past two years."

Becca turned to her new friend. "What happened?"

Abby let out a deep sigh. "Dr. Nick's wife died two years ago in a car crash. A terrible tragedy."

"Oh, my, I'm so sorry to hear that," Becca said. She took a deep breath as the pain of Dr. Nick's loss threatened to unearth her own.

"He's thrown himself into his work, the poor thing. Works all hours. He's renovated the stuffing out of the inside — turned it into a four-star resort for the cats and dogs and pigs and hamsters and iguanas he's rescued."

"Iguanas?" Becca said, startled.

Abby nodded. "All the creatures of the earth have a home with Dr. Nick." She took Becca by the arm. "Okay, it's getting pretty cold out here. Let's get inside."

Together they walked up the steps of the former mansion. Abby pushed open the big oak front door and ushered Becca into a warm, wood-paneled entry foyer decorated with wreaths of fir and cheery white Christmas lights. After the cold of the night outside — and it was night now, Becca realized, the sun having finally made its way below the horizon — the heat inside the house was welcome.

Becca's eyes were drawn from the foyer into a large room that had probably been the living room, back when the mansion was a family home. Now it was clearly the waiting room. In a corner, a woman with a short bob of white hair and an observant manner was sitting at a desk in front of a laptop, talking into a phone. Alerted by the gust of wintry air that pushed its way in behind Abby and Becca, the woman smiled when she saw Abby and waved them in.

Abby whispered to Becca, "That's Dr. Nick's business partner, Dr. Gail."

As they waited for Dr. Gail to finish on the phone, Becca took the chance to look around. During the day, she imagined the big tall windows flooded the room with tons of sunlight. There were plenty of chairs and even a couple of sofas for the humans and the animal patients. Becca was pleased that the chairs weren't like the impersonal office chairs that she saw so often when visiting the doctor or dentist. Instead, the chairs and side tables looked like they belonged in this grand old Victorian space.

As Becca stepped into the room, she turned and saw an entire wall covered in framed photographs. She gasped when she realized that each photo was of a pet and the pet's human family.

Abby stepped next to her. "All of these pets were rescues, and all of them have homes because of Dr. Nick and Dr. Gail."

The tears that had threatened Becca all day threatened her again. "This is wonderful," she said, reaching into her coat pocket for her handkerchief, her gaze wandering over the photos of smiling people with their happy pets. "Oh," she said, pointing to one photo of a cute little pink pig that seemed to be purring in bliss in his owner's arms. "A pig!"

"That's Pinkie the pot-bellied pig," Abby said. "My neighbors have him now. He's a bit headstrong, but a delightful pet. The kids love him."

Becca laughed. "Pinkie — what a great name!"

Across the room, Dr. Gail finished up on the phone, then stood and bustled toward them. She was a trim woman in her fifties, with a cheerful efficiency to her movements and manner.

"Abby, thank you for coming," Dr. Gail said, giving Abby a quick hug. Then she turned to Becca. "Let me guess. You're our new librarian."

Becca blushed. "I am. Becca Jameson. So pleased to meet you."

Dr. Gail took Becca's hand in hers. "Welcome to town. And in case you're wondering how I knew, I had advance notice. I was just on the phone with Bert Winters."

Abby said, "Bert wants to get the word out about the snowplow situation."

Dr. Gail nodded. "We'll tell the others. Everyone's downstairs in the kennels."

She led the way from the waiting room into a room that, once upon a time, was probably the mansion's dining room. The room was now set up as an examination room, with a big doctor's table in the center and walls lined with shelves of medical equipment and supplies.

Dr. Gail continued through swinging doors into the mansion's kitchen. This room still had the original farmhouse sink and counters and cabinets, but the ovens were gone — replaced with refrigerators — and the island prep space was now set up as a second examination table.

At the far end of the kitchen, a set of stairs descended down. Dr. Gail led the way into what had at one time been the grand home's basement.

Becca gave a small gasp. The space was now the kennel! Rows of spacious animal suites ran along both sides of the room. Everything was warmly lit and smelled of cleanliness and animals. And it wasn't the smell of animals in distress that Becca realized she was expecting. No, this space was filled with animals who knew they were in a good place. This was a place, she immediately understood, that was filled with caring and love. About half the suites were occupied with an assortment of dogs. She also saw a room filled with climbing ladders that several cats seemed to be enjoying.

The animals weren't the only ones there. In the center of the room, several volunteer workers looked on as a young family with two adorable children — a boy of four and a girl of two — played with an equally adorable terrier. The little dog was as excited as the two kids, wagging his tail and scampering about with a happiness exceeded only by the delight of the two kids.

"Looks like we have another match," Dr. Gail said with a smile.

Abby was looking around the kennel. "Where's Dr. Nick?"

"House call," Dr. Gail said. "Angus's mama llama isn't feeling well."

"Um, did you say *llama*?" Becca said.

Dr. Gail smiled. "Very sweet-natured creatures, unlike their camel cousins."

"You really do see it all, don't you?" Becca said, impressed.

"Young lady," Dr Gail said, "you wouldn't believe some of the things we've come across."

Becca grinned. She glanced at Abby and was surprised to see a dejected look on her new friend's face.

Becca said, "What's the matter, Abby?"

"Oh, nothing," Abby said, then added, with a glance at Dr. Gail, "I was looking forward to introducing Becca to Dr. Nick."

Dr. Gail gave Abby a knowing look. "Yes, I see what you mean," she said with a smile, then turned to Becca. "I'm sure you'll meet Nick soon enough. Now, let's introduce you to some of our residents."

CHAPTER 4

*B*ecca's heart leaped into her throat. *Meet the residents?* Already, the sight of the little terrier scampering about with the two children had left her feeling dangerously weakened. If she had any additional exposure to adorableness today, she was going to crumble!

"I don't know about this," Becca said, even as her traitorous eyes wandered toward the row of dog suites.

"Nonsense," Dr. Gail said. "No harm in looking." Without another word, she led Becca and Abby toward the animals.

No, doc, noooo! Becca wanted to say out loud. *I'm about as weak as it gets when it comes to cute animals!*

But the words never left her mouth. Her mouth dropped and her heart thumped, because right there in front of her, his tail wagging hopefully, was the fluffy white dog from the photo.

Dr. Gail smiled. "I see you recognize the star of today's event. Becca, I'd like to introduce you to Bowzer."

At the sound of his name, Bowzer shook with excitement.

Unable to stop herself, Becca knelt down in front of the kennel. "Hey, Bowzer. How are you?"

Bowzer gave her a joyful whimper, his tail wagging furiously.

"He likes you," Dr. Gail said. "Would you like to meet him?"

"Yes," Becca said helplessly, unable to stop herself, all thoughts about being strong dissolving away.

Dr. Gail unfastened the door of the kennel. Bowzer zoomed straight into Becca's arms, his fluffy white fur tickling her cheeks.

"Oh, my!" Becca said with a laugh. She gave the dog a hug, unable to stop herself, then looked up and found Abby and Dr. Gail grinning down at her.

"Abby," Becca said, "you were supposed to help me stay strong."

Abby laughed. "I think we both knew that wasn't going to happen."

Dr. Gail said, "Bowzer is two years old, part-mutt and part-English Sheepdog, and fully house-trained and leash-trained. His family had to give him up when they moved overseas for a new job. I promised them I'd find him a wonderful new home."

Becca looked at the adorable dog happily snuggling in her arms. "He's so friendly!"

"He has a marvelous disposition," Dr. Gail said. "He's had all his shots and tests."

"Oh, gosh," Becca said, "I just don't know." She gave Bowzer another hug, enjoying the fluffy warmth.

"I tell you what," Dr. Gail said. "Why don't the two of you get to know each other? I'll send him home with you for a couple of nights — we've got an overnight kit for him already prepared, with his favorite food and toys and contact information for me in case you have questions. If the two of you are a good fit, then come in after Christmas and we'll get everything settled."

Abby said, "I like the sound of that, Becca. A trial run for both of you."

Becca sighed. She liked the sound of it, too — she liked it *a lot*. Already, she knew exactly what was going to happen. She and Bowzer would bond and become inseparable and Becca's plan to be strong and realistic and sensible would be doomed to utter failure!

Bowzer chose that moment to lick Becca's cheek, and Becca laughed.

"Fine," she said, then laughed again. "I'll spend Christmas with Bowzer."

"Hurray!" Abby said.

"Congratulations, Becca," Dr. Gail said. "I can tell that the two of you are going to get along wonderfully."

Becca stood up and gave Abby a pretend-glare. "This is all your fault!"

Abby laughed. "Guilty as charged."

Dr. Gail pointed to a container filled with a three-day supply of dog food and dog treats. "If you'd like, I'll swing by your cottage with Bowzer's overnight kit after I close up here."

"You know where I live?" Becca said.

"You're renting the little Cape Cod-style white cottage on Pine Street, right?"

"Everyone here seems to know everything about me," Becca said.

"Only the basics, Becca," Dr. Gail said. "New librarian. Cape Cod cottage. Loves dogs."

"And loves chocolate!" Abby added.

Becca grinned at her new friends. "Well, there are two more things you should know about me. One: I'm very happy I've met the two of you — excuse me, the three of you," she said, reaching down to give Bowzer an affectionate pat.

"And two: I'm very happy I made the move to Heartsprings Valley!"

CHAPTER 5

*a*nd she was happy about moving here, Becca realized, as she sat that evening on her comfy sofa in her cozy cottage next to her new canine roommate, surrounded by a room full of boxes she would eventually need to unpack. The day's rush of new experiences flooded over her, causing her to take a deep breath. Meeting Abby, Bert, Dr. Gail and of course Bowzer had been both fun and a little exhausting!

Change was never easy, even when the change was necessary and good. She'd always been the cautious type — curious about the world, but measured in how she approached new people or challenges. She couldn't think of the last time she'd met so many new people in a single day. But from the way her spirits lifted when she thought about them all, she knew again she'd made the right choice by deciding to strike out on her own.

The people of this small New England town were so welcoming. But they were also clever. She sensed they had plans for her. She still wasn't quite sure how Abby and Dr. Gail had maneuvered her into adopting Bowzer. If she didn't stay on her toes, she'd soon be adopting an entire menagerie!

She smiled at the thought of that, happy that her weakness for animals had defeated her oh-so-reasonable intention to be strong. Sometimes, matters of the heart were more important than proving that one had the ability to follow some pre-set plan. Next to her, Bowzer wagged his tail happily as he chewed on a toy.

Even though part of her was bone-tired and longed for a nap on her comfy couch, another part of her felt restless, even — dare she say it? — surprisingly peppy. "Is that because of you, Bowzer?" she said to her new companion, who perked up at the sound of his name. "You're like an energy battery, aren't you?"

Maybe, she thought, casting her eye around her cozy living room, she should tackle some of the tasks she'd been avoiding since moving into her cottage two days earlier. Her to-do list was about a mile long! The movers had arrived the day before with her bed and sofa and chest of drawers and dining table and chairs, so at least she had places to sit and sleep. Here in the living room, she'd positioned her big leather sofa in front of the big window. Opposite her was the gas fireplace, which she'd promptly turned on as soon as she'd arrived home. Very quickly, the fireplace had turned the room toasty warm.

As for the rest of the living room: Boxes everywhere! Oh, she had so much to do.

She sighed. "Okay, Bowzer. Which box first?"

Bowzer gave her an encouraging bark.

"Got it," she said. "Linens and blankets it is." She eased off the couch and pulled a big box toward her. With a few deft movements, the packing tape was gone and the lid of the box flew open.

She reached in. A heavy warm blue blanket, a blend of cotton and wool, emerged first. "You go on the couch," she said as she set the blanket next to Bowzer.

She reached down again and pulled out what she'd really been looking for: the red-and-green Christmas quilt her beloved Grandma Ellie had made for her years ago. She unfolded the quilt and held it in front of her so that she could once again feast her eyes on it. She'd always loved this quilt. The patterns were a cornucopia of every-thing that represented Christmas to her. Ginger-bread men, Christmas trees, snow sculptures, reindeer flying a sleigh across the night sky — all were there. In the center, a hand-stitched message that even now, twenty years later, brought a lump to her throat: "Merry Christmas, Becca! Love you forever, Grandma Ellie."

She looked at the quilt and said, "You need a place of honor."

But where? Right now, she had nothing hanging on the walls, and nothing to hang up things with.

Ah — she had the perfect spot. She stood up and turned around and lovingly draped the quilt over the back of the sofa. Just this simple act turned the room from "moving-in messy" to "Christmas-time comfortable." A smile crept to her lips as she took in the full picture of Bowzer happily chewing his toy on the sofa decorated with Grandma's Christmas quilt.

On an impulse, she snapped a photo of the scene and texted it to her mom with a message: "Meet Bowzer!"

Oh, gosh — what was her mother going to say?

Seconds later, her phone rang and she found out.

"Hi, Mom!" Becca said.

"Becca," her mother said, "who is Bowzer? Is Bowzer the dog? Does your message mean what I think it means?"

"I adopted him, Mom. The vet had a pet adoption event."

Her mom was momentarily speechless, and Becca knew why — her mom was torn between congratulating her and warning her that now was the time to be responsible and careful, not impulsive.

Becca said, "He's adorable, Mom. His name is Bowzer, and he's very sweet. He's two years old, he's fully house-trained, and he's had all his shots and tests."

"Well, dear, I..." her mom said. "I suppose congratulations are in order."

"I couldn't help myself, Mom. There was a sign in the display window of the chocolate store, and I saw Bowzer's picture, and I don't know what came over me."

"Well, he certainly looks adorable. What kind of dog is he?"

"The vet says he's part-mutt and part-English Sheepdog."

She heard her mother say to someone, "Becca adopted a dog!" Then: "Two years old. House-trained. An English Sheepdog-mutt mix." Then: "Becca, your father said congratulations."

Becca smiled. "Dad approves?"

"Of course he approves — when it comes to animals, he's as big a softie as you are!"

There was a pause, and then her mom said, "How are *you* doing, dear?"

"So far, so good. I met some really nice people today. Everyone here is so welcoming." She told her mom about her busy day — her afternoon with Hettie Mae at the library, meeting Abby at the chocolate shop, meeting Bert in the town square, and going to the veterinary clinic and meeting Dr. Gail.

Her mom asked all kinds of questions, as her mom was inclined to do.

"Have you unpacked yet?" her mom asked.

"Hardly at all. I just opened the linen box and pulled out Grandma's quilt and draped it over the sofa right before I sent you the photo."

"Have you opened the box marked 'Surprise!'?"

A box with a surprise? Becca's pulse quickened. "No, I didn't even notice it. Let me look." She walked to the stack of unopened boxes on one side of the room. It took her a couple of seconds, but she found the box.

"Mom, what's in it?" she said with a smile on her face.

"You'll have to open it to find out," her mom said with a teasing lilt.

"Okay, let me put down the phone." She pressed the phone's speaker button and set the phone on the arm of the couch, then picked up the box and set it down on the couch next to Bowzer.

Eagerly she ripped the box open, then lifted the lid and peered inside and gasped.

"Oh, mom — Christmas decorations!"

Inside the box was a colorful, glittering explosion of holiday goodness — ornaments and mementos that brought back cherished moments from her childhood. She picked up a snow globe she'd owned ever since she was a little girl and gave it a shake, smiling as she watched the snow swirl and settle over the cute little town inside.

For the third time that day, tears filled her eyes. "Mom, you shouldn't have. This is so beautiful."

"Even though you're alone up there, I want you to feel the Christmas spirit," her mom said. "Your dad and brothers and I are thinking about you every minute."

Becca wiped away grateful tears. "I'm going to decorate the cottage right away."

"Good!"

Bowzer joined in with a short joyful bark.

"Is Bowzer going to help you?" her mom said with a laugh.

"He sure is. He's helped so much already."

"That's good, dear. Oh, gosh, I have to get a pie out of the oven. Call tomorrow, okay?"

"Of course. I love you, mom."

"I love you, too."

CHAPTER 6

*I*nspired by her mom's surprise gift, Becca dove right into the decorating. First out of the box was a long train of silver tinsel, which she used to frame the doorway between the living room and the kitchen. Next came the ornaments — more than a dozen of them, lovingly selected by her mom. She smiled as she took out each one, memories flooding through her.

She picked up one her favorites — a Christmas tree ornament, sparkling with green and gold glitter. She and her younger brother Bobby had competed for years to see who got to hang it on the tree. She tried to remember who had won that annual competition most often — she thought it was her, by a nose.

Next up was the reindeer her dad had carved

from a piece of driftwood he'd found during a summer vacation at the beach. After carving the wood into the shape of a reindeer flying through the sky, he'd painted it with a red nose and big smile. He'd done that in his workshop in the garage over a rainy weekend one fall when she was eight or nine, while she'd watched, chattering happily away as he carefully shaped the wood.

Next out was a silver globe that she herself had painted when she was in the third grade. The words, "Merry Christmas" in red paint, looked blocky and awkward and shaky — she'd been eight years old, after all! — but they also reminded her how seriously she'd applied herself to the task at hand, and how proud she'd been of the result.

And then — her breath caught. Bowzer noticed and looked up. The ornament she took from the box had been sent to her by her husband Dave during his deployment to Afghanistan. Somehow, he'd found time in his insanely busy schedule to have a special ornament designed and made and sent to her. The ornament was in the shape of a home, with a picture of Dave and Becca inside pressed glass. The photo was from their wedding — the two of them feeding each other bites of their wedding cake. They both looked so happy, so full of hope, so optimistic.

Inscribed on the glass was a single word: "Forever."

Her throat tightened. Forever hadn't happened, not for them. A landmine buried in the sands of that far-off country had seen to that. Instantly, irrevocably, life as she'd known it was obliterated.

Nearly three years had passed since that awful day. She knew her grief would be with her, always. He'd been her everything, her life, her future, until in the blink of an eye he was gone. The first two Christmases without him had been wrenching and so utterly painful — she'd been such an emotional wreck, despite trying to put on a brave face. Her family had tried to lighten her spirits, tried to distract her, tried to cheer her up, tried to keep her so busy with holiday activities that she wouldn't have time to dwell on what she'd lost. Her family loved her and wanted what was best for her and meant well, but they would never be able to truly understand what she was experiencing, because none of them had had the devastating misfortune of losing a spouse in war. None of them understood that, for her, her nearly three years of grieving were what she *needed* to go through if she was ever going to have a prayer of moving forward and learning again how to *live* the rest of her life and not merely exist.

She heard a whimper and turned to Bowzer,

who was looking at her with sympathy. His tail wagged slowly and he whimpered again.

"Oh, Bowzer," she said as she sat herself down next to him on the couch and wrapped him in a hug. "You are such a smart dog. Yes, momma's a bit down. But not for long."

She sat up, squared her shoulders, and stood up. "Your momma's ready for a change. A new town, new job, and new beginning." She turned to Bowzer. "And new you!"

Bowzer barked in agreement.

"Now," she said, taking a deep breath and eyeing the pile of boxes, "time for some serious unpacking!"

CHAPTER 7

*B*ecca awoke the next morning to the warmth of the sun on her cheeks from the bright winter light streaming through her bedroom window. She stretched her arms under her cozy comforter and groaned — oh, how her arms and shoulders ached! Moving and unpacking those boxes had been a lot of work. She was going to be one sore girl today.

She glanced at her bedside clock. It was a bit after eight in the morning. And today was — Christmas Eve! Immediately, she shot straight up in the bed, the covers tumbling away. She had so much to do today.

But first things first: time for Bowzer to do his business!

Her new canine companion, alerted to the

sound of her feet hitting the floor, bounded into her bedroom and greeted her with a happy bark. He rushed into her outstretched arms.

"Good morning, boy," she said as she gave him an affectionate cuddle. "Let's get you outside."

Without even a thought about how she looked in her pajamas and tousled hair, she walked into the living room, slipped into her winter boots, then grabbed her heavy winter coat and scarf and gloves and threw them on.

She picked up the leash and turned to Bowzer. "How about a quick walk now, and then a longer walk later?" she said.

Tail wagging, Bowzer waited patiently while she fastened the leash to his collar. The instant it was on, he tugged her determinedly toward the front door.

With a laugh, Becca pulled open the door and felt an icy *whoosh* as frigid winter air rushed over her.

"Oh, my!" she said, shocked at the sharp crispness. "It's so cold!" She laughed again as Bowzer dragged her with him down the short path in front of her cottage to the sidewalk that ran along her street. Eagerly, his nose vibrating with pleasure, he began a thorough examination of his new neighborhood, stopping at every tree he passed to sniff very carefully.

So much of what a dog sensed about the world was from their extraordinary sense of smell. She wondered what her world would be like if her own nose was that sensitive. There were, of course, lots of smells she had zero interest in, thank you very much! But to be able to dive into, indulge in, roll around in and revel in, the smell of coffee and hot cocoa and gingerbread cookies and her mom's famous apple pie — that would be heavenly.

The icy air whipping around her pajama-clad legs made her realize that, even with her boots and heavy coat and scarf, she was not dressed to be out in this weather. As a newcomer to Heartsprings Valley, she was going to have to make some wardrobe adjustments. She thought longingly about the warmth of her cozy cottage, but Bowzer seemed so excited and happy and focused — like an investigator on the prowl of a scent — that she willingly let him lead her up the street for a few more minutes.

The other houses on Pine Street were charming and well-kept (though not as adorable as her cottage, she thought loyally), and most of them were strung up with Christmas lights and festooned with decorations celebrating the season. Through several windows, she saw families moving around. The morning sunlight reflected off the snow on the ground so brightly that she found herself wishing she'd brought a pair of sunglasses to wear.

Bowzer looked up at her inquiringly when he reached the end of the street. A path led toward what looked like a meadow, and beyond the meadow, Becca caught a glimpse of Heartsprings Lake. She'd passed the lake several times, but she hadn't had time yet to go to the shoreline for a visit.

"How about a nice long walk this afternoon?" she said to Bowzer. "After we start on the ginger-bread cookies, okay?"

Bowzer gazed wistfully toward the lake, but he didn't make a fuss when she turned them around and headed back to their new home.

When they reached the cottage, she paused for a moment to admire its appearance. She'd loved how it looked in the photos that Hettie Mae had sent, but she had to admit, the real-life version looked even better. On the outside, it was painted with colors that were perfect for Christmas, with creamy white clapboard siding and windows trimmed in red. The green pine trees that rose next to the house completed the holiday color scheme. Hettie Mae had even bought her a housewarming gift — a wreath of Balsam that now hung from the cottage's red front door.

Becca was in danger of losing herself in appreciation of her new home's exterior when a gust of air against her pajama-clad legs reminded her that it was winter. *Brrrr!* With Bowzer in tow, she bustled to the front door and scooted inside.

She unfastened Bowzer's leash and hung it on a coat hook near the door, then slid off her winter coat and scarf. After hanging them on a hook next to the leash, she reached down and slipped off her boots and put on her slippers.

Her new home was still a bit of a mess, she thought with a frown as she surveyed the living room. A mountain of boxes still needed to be unpacked despite the dent she'd made in them the previous evening. She made her way into the kitchen, which had recently been updated with stainless steel appliances, grey granite counter-tops, and creamy white cabinets that beautifully matched the big farmer's sink under the window overlooking her cute little backyard.

The kitchen wasn't big, but it had plenty of counter space. It also boasted a sunny breakfast nook flooded with morning light. Becca had been thrilled to discover that her small round oak dining table and four dining chairs fit perfectly in the space.

For tomorrow's Christmas Day dinner at Hettie Mae's, Becca had decided to make a small gingerbread house. She'd always been drawn to the intricacy of that particular holiday activity. The wonderful aroma of the gingerbread as it emerged from the oven never failed to transport her back to her childhood, when her mom and grandmother had helped her make her very first gingerbread masterpiece. Every aspect of the house-building brought her pleasure — kneading the dough, shaping the gingerbread into the right shapes and sizes for the home's walls and roof, gluing the pieces together with frosting, and then — and this was her favorite part — decorating! Maybe, if she hadn't fallen in love with books and libraries, she might have been an architect or an interior designer. She nearly laughed out loud at the thought of making a life-size, real-world gingerbread house to live in.

She turned on the radio and sighed as holiday music filled the room. She enjoyed many kinds of music, but the traditional songs of Christmas held a special place in her heart. Just the thought of the familiar songs and lyrics brought a smile to her lips.

Humming along, she reviewed her plan for the day. The library was closed today, and Hettie Mae had been extremely firm about Becca not setting foot in the library until the day after Christmas. And while her unpacked boxes beckoned, there was no hurry on that front either.

Nope, today she was going to indulge herself.

First she'd make the dough for the gingerbread cookies and let it sit. Then, after cleaning up and making herself presentable, she'd take Bowzer on a nice long afternoon walk to explore her new town. Later on, when she got home, she'd put the gingerbread in the oven, make the frosting, and spend her evening decorating her gingerbread house.

And maybe, just maybe, she'd unpack a few more boxes before she went to bed that night.

At that very moment, her phone rang. She picked it up, not recognizing the number. "Hello?" she said.

"Becca, it's Dr. Gail."

"Hi, how are you?" Becca said, pleased to hear the veterinarian's voice.

"I'm calling to check in on you and Bowzer."

"Bowzer and I are doing great. He's such a sweetheart. We just got back from a walk."

"Glad to hear that," Dr. Gail said. "Everything going well so far?"

"It's going wonderfully."

"Good. I'm so pleased to hear that. I meant to ask yesterday, do you have plans for Christmas Day? We're hosting a Christmas gathering at the clinic tomorrow afternoon starting at 4 p.m., a potluck of sorts, and we'd love to have you join us."

"Oh, thank you so much," Becca said, touched

by the vet's thoughtfulness. "Hettie Mae has invited me to her house for Christmas dinner, so I'm covered."

"Oh, that's wonderful. Hettie Mae makes the most delicious scalloped potatoes — you'll love them."

Becca laughed, and Bowzer chose that moment to wander into the kitchen. He barked happily in response to Becca's laugh.

Dr. Gail said, "Is that Bowzer I hear?"

"Sure is. He doesn't know it yet, but he's going to help me make gingerbread cookie dough before we go on a long walk this afternoon."

Dr. Gail laughed. "I'll let you get to it. Merry Christmas, Becca."

"Merry Christmas to you!"

Becca set down the phone and turned to Bowzer, who looked up at her with an eager expression.

"Have you ever made gingerbread, Bowzer?"

Bowzer gave her a puzzled yet hopeful look.

"No, not yet? But you can't wait to get started? Good boy!"

Becca reached into Bowzer's overnight kit and pulled out a chew bone. Bowzer whined and pawed the floor with anticipation.

"Here you go, boy!" With a toss, the bone flew through the air and landed in the middle of Bowzer's day bed next to the dining table.

Happily, Bowzer bounded to his day bed and settled in for a good long chew.

CHAPTER 8

$\mathcal{B}$ecca smiled as she watched her new companion lose himself in the simple enjoyment of chewing his toy. Oh, to live a dog's life!

With Bowzer settled, it was time for her to get busy with one of her favorite holiday traditions. She ran her hand over the grey granite countertop and realized she had not yet cooked or baked anything in her new kitchen. How appropriate that her very first culinary endeavor in her new cottage would be her very favorite baking activity.

As she had discovered when she moved in, her new kitchen had wonderful storage and lovely cabinet drawers that slid in and out with a simple touch. Cooking and baking and preparing meals in this space was going to be so enjoyable

— quite unlike some of the kitchens she'd dealt with. She remembered her first kitchen as a grownup, in the ratty old house she and Dave moved into as budget-conscious newlyweds after their wedding. The kitchen in that house had been rundown and dated, and creaky and cranky to boot. One cabinet drawer had simply refused to stay shut. Every time she turned around, the drawer seemed to slide out another inch! She'd joked that a ghost lived in the drawer and needed fresh air.

The kitchen in her new cottage didn't pose any such concerns, thankfully. Everything here was up-to-date and modern, while retaining its traditional charm. The only ghost in this kitchen was the spirit of the Christmas season, welcoming her to the cottage and to Heartsprings Valley.

She blinked as she realized that her mom was probably in her own kitchen at this very moment, happily prepping the turkey or making stuffing from scratch or laying apple slices into a pie. She felt a tug of longing for her childhood home and wondered again if her decision to move to Heartsprings Valley before Christmas had been the right call for her.

A second vision appeared in her head — a picture of what the gingerbread house she was going to make would look like. It would be a charming Cape Cod-style cottage, clad in creamy white, with red-trimmed windows and a wreath on the red front door.

"A gingerbread version of my beautiful cottage," she said to herself, a smile on her face.

Eagerly, she opened the big cabinet next to the fridge and began pulling out the ingredients she'd bought when she'd arrived in town. She'd made gingerbread cookies so many times over the years that she had the recipe memorized. In a flash, she gathered the ingredients and lined them up on the counter, ready and waiting. Flour, check. Baking soda, cinnamon, and salt — check, check, check. Cloves and ginger — double check.

She opened a lower storage drawer next to her sink and took out two mixing bowls and a cooking pan. Then, from another drawer, came her mixer — a birthday gift from her mom. Then, from her utensils drawer, she took out her rolling pin and measuring cups and spoons.

She paused for a moment before beginning. All she was doing was making gingerbread — an activity she'd done a thousand times — yet somehow this occasion felt more meaningful. She'd moved on her own to a town where everyone was a stranger. She was starting a new job that would put her in charge of a library. She'd rented a cottage, sight unseen, from photos sent in an email. She'd impulsively adopted a dog.

Pure craziness!

And yet, as she gazed at the ingredients on her kitchen counter and prepared to make a gingerbread house based on her new home, she felt a surge of emotion. What she'd done felt so *right*.

She scooped up a cup of flour and dropped it into the mixing bowl, then added the baking soda, cinnamon, and salt. She stirred a bit, added the ginger and cloves, and stirred some more.

Setting aside the dry bowl, she grabbed the mixing bowl, added butter and brown sugar, then added the eggs in one at a time. She placed the bowl under her mixer, set it on medium, and hit the "on" switch. With a whir, the mixer started creaming the eggs and sugar and butter. She added in lemon zest, molasses and vanilla, enjoying the lovely smells of each.

When the consistency looked right, she picked up the bowl of dry ingredients and added them gradually. When the mixer started straining against the thickening dough, Becca hit the "off" switch and removed the bowl from the mixer. She rinsed her hands in the sink, then reached into the bowl and kneaded the dough with both hands for a good long minute.

She looked around her counter. Where was

her wax paper? She rinsed her hands again, then proceeded to open several cabinets until she found where she'd put the wax paper roll. Was that cabinet where she wanted to keep it? She paused, considering, then nodded. Yes, that cabinet was fine.

She rolled out three good-size lengths of wax paper, then reached into the bowl and divided the dough into three chunks: two big chunks, each of which she wrapped in the wax paper and set in the fridge. She sighed happily, already antici-pating her evening activity of house-building and decorating.

But as for the final chunk of dough…. Even though the dough ideally needed to sit for at least a couple of hours, she couldn't resist taking a small chunk and rolling it out immediately. These few cookies would be just for her, so it didn't matter if they came out less than perfect.

She sprinkled flour on the rolling board, on her rolling pin, and then on the dough. She set the dough on the board and started rolling, putting in some muscle!

A minute later, the dough was a quarter-inch thick and perfect for the next step. She picked up her preferred cutout — a gingerbread man, of course — and started pressing it into the dough. The dough yielded four cookies. Another round of rolling yielded two more gingerbread cookies for the cookie sheet.

She picked up the cookie sheet and slid it into the oven. Oh, she could barely wait! In eight minutes, she knew, the cookies would be ready — soft and delicious and irresistible.

She should be strong, she told herself. When the cookies came out of the oven, she should let them cool. She should leave them be, let them lie undisturbed, so that she could decorate them this evening, after she got back from her walk with Bowzer. Yes, that's what a strong person would do.

But who was she kidding? Those cookies — at least a few of them — weren't going to survive long enough to be decorated. Becca's stomach chose that moment to rumble in agreement. Those cookies were doomed!

CHAPTER 9

*a*n hour later, the wonderful smell of the two surviving gingerbread cookies still fresh in the air, Becca gave herself one last look in her bathroom mirror before going out. She'd always been a list person, so she mentally reviewed her appearance:

Shoulder-length brown hair, a bit curlier than she would have liked, but still looking bouncy and clean after her shower: Check.

A hint of foundation on her cheeks to even out her complexion: Check.

A soft red lip balm, subtle rather than bold, to help protect her lips from the cold air outside: Check.

Her favorite burgundy turtleneck sweater, the one that somehow made her look a bit taller and a bit slimmer than her very average height and weight: Check.

Her new navy-blue ski pants, purchased for her move to Heartsprings Valley, which were not only wonderfully warm but which somehow made her legs look a bit longer than they really were: Check.

Yes, she thought, giving herself a final review, she was ready to face the world. At least as ready as she could be, here in this new town.

She touched the ring on the third finger of her left hand. A simple silver band with a single diamond. Even now it shone brightly.

She turned her head from side to side and pushed back her hair to make sure the silver reindeer earrings — a Christmas gift from her mom and dad — hadn't fallen off.

One last thing. She test-smiled and leaned closer to make sure she didn't have anything stuck between her teeth. She'd learned from hard-won experience how important this step was.

Clean teeth: Check!

Okay, she told herself, *let's do this.* She gave herself a nod, then left the bathroom and marched into the living room, where Bowzer was waiting patiently.

"Bowzer," she said, "you ready for a long walk?"

With an eager whine, her canine companion

leaped to his feet and stretched and shook himself in anticipation.

She smiled as she slid into her comfy black winter boots. She put on her black winter gloves, then grabbed her red paisley scarf and wrapped it around her neck. Instantly she felt its comforting warmth against her skin.

As she shrugged into her thick dark-blue winter coat, she realized she was extremely bundled up. Maybe too bundled up? After all, the afternoon sun was shining brightly, and the town was small. Even if she got cold, the warmth and comfort of her cozy cottage would never be more than a short walk away. Could she leave some of her layers at home?

"Nope, better safe than sorry," she said to Bowzer, who'd been watching her with barely restrained impatience. "What about you? Are you going to be warm?"

Her gaze fell on Bowzer's shaggy white coat, which was built for wintry conditions. "Of course you're going to be warm," she said to him. "Just look at you!"

With a final check to make sure her wallet and phone were in her coat pocket, she bent down with the leash and hooked it to Bowzer's collar.

"Ready, boy?"

With a happy bark, Bowzer pulled her to the door, which she promptly opened.

And they were off! Becca breathed in sharply as she adjusted to the crisp winter afternoon air. The sun above cast bright light on everything, with the reflection on the snow causing her to squint and remember —

"Sunglasses!" she said out loud. She stopped in her tracks and tried to recall where she'd left them. After a second, she got it: On the kitchen counter, in the change basket next to the fridge.

"One second, Bowzer." She turned around and opened her red front door and bustled into the kitchen and found her glasses and slipped them on. Yes, much better. The smell of the gingerbread cookies was so wonderful that she couldn't resist: She leaned closer to the two surviving cookies on the wire rack and breathed in the wonderful aroma. Weakened even further, she picked one up. The gingerbread man was bare of decorations, but in that moment, she didn't care.

"Sorry, little guy, momma's hungry and she's got a big walk ahead of her."

She bit his head off — yummmm — and reveled in the wonderful taste. His legs and arms quickly found their way into her mouth, followed at last by his torso.

"Yum," she said to Bowzer, who gave her an impatient bark.

She laughed, her mouth still full of gingerbread man, and said, "Yes, Bowzer, you're abso-lutely right, I need to stop eating these cookies!"

Without another second's delay, she marched back out the door, shut it firmly behind her, and aimed herself forward.

Onward ho!

CHAPTER 10

The mid-afternoon winter sun was bright overhead as Becca and Bowzer made their way to the end of Pine Street and stepped onto the path that led to the meadow near Heartsprings Lake. A crisp gust of wind blew against her cheeks as her boots crunched through the snow. The ground wasn't icy, but she made sure she paid careful attention to her steps. The last thing she wanted was an unanticipated spill.

Bowzer had no such worries. Excitedly, his nose sniffing at every bush and tree, he pulled her forward.

The path leading to the meadow wound gently through a stand of pine trees. Sunlight dappled the snow already coating the ground.

Though cold, the air seemed milder here amidst the trees, protected from the winds.

That protection vanished the instant she and Bowzer emerged onto the open meadow. A rush of air caused her to gasp. *Brrr!*

"It's so cold, Bowzer," she said to her companion, who was too busy sniffing the ground to pay any attention.

The meadow gently sloped upward to a crest. When Becca reached the high point of the meadow, she stopped and gasped again as she was treated to the glorious vista of Heartsprings Lake before her. The lake, nestled on either side by mountains, was dazzling, the sunlight reflecting off its frozen surface, making her very happy she'd remembered to bring her sunglasses. The lake wasn't large, but it certainly was beautiful. She'd read that in the summer months it was a favorite of waterskiers and boaters and fishermen.

But now, with winter upon them, she saw a different activity in full swing: ice skating! She smiled as she gazed upon a dozen or more skaters flying across the surface of the frozen lake. Some of the skaters looked like beginners, their movements tentative and awkward, while others danced effortlessly across the ice, their smooth gliding a testament to their experience and skill.

Like her, the skaters were bundled up for winter. She zeroed in one of the skillful skaters and realized it was Bert Winters, whom she had met the day before in the town square. She remembered how Abby had described him — "Mr. Everything" — and smiled.

"Come on, Bowzer," she said. Eagerly, the two of them followed the path down the meadow to the shore of the lake.

Bert saw her, waved, and zoomed up to the edge of the shore. "Good afternoon, young lady," he boomed, a grin on his face.

"Afternoon to you, Bert. Merry Christmas!"

"Merry Christmas! I understand you'll be at Hettie Mae's tomorrow."

"Absolutely."

"Good, good." His eyes swung to Bowzer. "I see that Dr. Gail introduced you to Bowzer."

"She sure did. I think she and Abby had a secret plan to get me to adopt him."

Bert chuckled. "That wouldn't surprise me at all. Is that what you'll be doing? Adopting him?"

"Yes. I never thought I'd find myself in this situation, especially not so soon after moving here, but...." She reached down and gave Bowzer a pat. "How could I resist?"

"That's the spirit."

"We're taking an afternoon walk. Any suggestions?"

"There are wonderful walking paths on the ridge above the lake that I'd recommend. A few of them rise high enough to provide incredible views of the lake. But maybe not today, not with the —"

Bert's attention was diverted at that moment by a child's cry. The two of them turned and saw that a boy, about six years old, had fallen on the ice and was shaken up.

"My grandson Charlie," he said. "I better get over there and help."

"Is he okay?" she asked anxiously.

"He's fine," he said, eyeing him expertly. "He just needs a little reassurance and a helping hand."

"Great seeing you, Bert. Merry Christmas!"

"Merry Christmas, Becca!" Bert said as he skated away.

CHAPTER 11

*B*ecca watched from the edge of the lake as Bert helped his grandson back onto his feet. The two of them talked for a minute as Bert wiped tears from the boy's face and helped him blow his nose. Bert held out his hand and said something, and the boy nodded. Taking hold of his grandfather's hand, the boy started moving forward on his skates again, tentatively at first, then with greater confidence. After a minute of holding tight, he let go and set out on his own, his little legs pushing him faster and faster across the ice.

Family was so important, Becca thought. She'd been so lucky growing up in her family, and Christmas always reminded her of that essential truth.

Bowzer chose that moment to nuzzle her leg.

She glanced down at her new canine companion, who returned her gaze with a hopeful expression.

"You ready for more exploring, Bowzer?" she said.

He gave her an encouraging bark, and the two of them continued along the shoreline, enjoying the afternoon air and the heartwarming sight of skaters flying across the ice.

Ahead of her, she noticed a sign that said, "Ridge Trail." Bert had mentioned the trails and the views of the valley. She looked back toward Bert to see if she could ask him more, but she saw he was far out on the lake now, skating after his energetic (and now very confident) grandson.

She turned to Bowzer. "Why don't we see where the trail takes us? What do you say?"

Bowzer barked his agreement. With a rush of pleasure at how adventurous she was feeling, she led Bowzer onto the trail. The snow on the path wasn't thick at all — an inch or two at most — and felt soft and fluffy. The slight crunch under her booted feet gave her a sense of comfort that she wasn't likely to encounter icy or slippery conditions. She knew from experience that if anyone was likely to tumble on icy ground, it was her.

The air was so fresh, with a hint of snow and pine. She breathed in deeply.

"It's so beautiful, isn't it?" she said to Bowzer,

who was too busy sniffing the base of a tree to agree.

The trail wound gently in a switchback pattern up the mountain. At every turn in the path, evergreen trees greeted her, snow dusting their branches. Aside from the sound of the breeze rustling through the trees and the occasional panting of her companion, the mountain trail was wonderfully quiet.

A squawk from above caused her to look up into the blue sky, where she spied a hawk soaring, its wings spread to catch the air.

Even though she wasn't tired or even breathing heavily, she knew she'd be tuckered out after today's walk. The exercise was good for her, she told herself. Filling her lungs with fresh air, stretching her legs on a nice hike, enjoying a beautiful day with a happy dog — was there a better way to spend an afternoon?

She'd been climbing for a good twenty minutes when she reached a turn that opened to a view of the lake below. She stopped and gasped.

It was so beautiful! The lake stretched out below her, hugged on all sides by mountains covered with lush stands of evergreen trees dusted with snow. Below her, skaters dashed and danced across the ice. On the shore, she saw that a number of folks were taking off their skates and getting ready to head back home. They all looked so tiny from where she stood — like miniature figures in a snow globe. She was just able to make out Bert and his grandson on the shore, where Bert was helping remove a skate from his grandson's foot.

From where she stood on the trail, she also had a view of the meadow that she and Bowzer had walked across, along with a view of the edge of her neighborhood.

But she couldn't see her own cottage or the town square of Heartsprings Valley itself — not from where she was standing right now. She looked up the ridge and noticed, further up, a viewing spot that appeared to offer a more commanding view.

"Come on, Bowzer," she said. "Momma wants to see what our cottage looks like from higher up."

Always happy to explore more, Bowzer bounded forward, his eagerness helping to tug her up the path. After a few minutes, they reached a fork in the path, with one path following the ridge above the lake and the other heading toward what looked like a pass to the back side of the ridge. A few minutes later, they reached a second fork, again with one path following the ridge along the lake.

After a few more minutes of climbing, she realized that the panting she heard wasn't from

Bowzer, but from her. The path had gotten steeper as they'd climbed higher. Her gentle afternoon stroll had turned into a real workout!

The wind was picking up now, the breeze rustling the tops of the trees. A dash of wintry air swept across her cheeks, which, she expected, were now rosy-red from the cold. But her goal wasn't far, she sensed.

"Come on, Bowzer," she said, picking up her pace. "We're almost there."

Another bend in the trail and yet another fork appeared, but she pressed on, her breath and Bowzer's puffing away as they pushed closer and closer to their goal.

Finally, after a steep stretch of trail that really got her legs burning with exertion, she reached the spot she'd seen.

And what she was able to see from her spot high on the ridge overlooking the valley was — glorious! Below her was a panoramic view of Heartsprings Valley. The town looked so wonderful from this vantage point — the very essence of small-town New England. She was able to pick out the town square, and even the top of the bandstand in the center of the square. A block away, she saw the rooftop turrets of the veterinary clinic where she and Bowzer had found each other. Just a few blocks from there, she knew, was her quaint neighborhood. She couldn't see her cozy cottage — the surrounding trees blocked the view — but she smiled and felt comforted knowing it was there.

On the snow-covered meadow next to the lake, she noticed folks heading back to town after their afternoon of ice-skating. As her gaze wandered toward the lake itself, she realized that all of the skaters had called it a day.

She frowned. It was almost like they'd all decided to leave at the same time. But why would they do that? She glanced at the mountains on the other side of the lake, and on the horizon she saw why. Huge dark clouds were bearing down from the east.

A gust of arctic air hit her then, like a warning, and Bowzer whimpered. She recalled what Bert and Abby had said the previous day: A nor'easter was coming. She had assumed, from the way they were talking, that a nor'easter was not to be taken lightly. And my, those clouds looked angry and ominous.

Another blast of wind hit her and she gasped. It was time to head home — time to get her and Bowzer safely ensconced in their cozy cottage.

But even as that thought planted itself in her mind, she couldn't help but stand still for a few seconds more and watch, transfixed, as the advancing storm swept over the mountains on the other side of the lake. There was a terrible beauty to the fury of the approaching blizzard. It seemed to roll forward like a relentless wave. The mountains on the other side of the lake disappeared as the dark angry clouds raced toward her.

The storm was moving so fast! Within seconds, it seemed, the lake had vanished as well, lost amidst a swirling maelstrom of snow and wind.

With a mixture of awe and mounting fear, she watched the storm reach her side of the lake. For just a few seconds more, the sun was still above her and she could see the town below her, but then —

Pow!

CHAPTER 12

With a roar, the storm was upon them. She gasped and Bowzer barked in bewilderment as they were surrounded by swirling winds and blinding snow. The bright afternoon sun vanished, replaced by a dim grayness. The storm's fury lashed against them. Instead of being able to see for miles, visibility dropped to mere yards.

She needed to get herself and Bowzer down off this mountain — pronto! Which meant getting back to the lake. Once she got down the mountain, she knew she could find her way home.

"Come on, Bowzer," she said, urgency in her voice. "Let's get out of here!"

Her companion needed no persuasion. With a determined gait, he headed back toward where they'd come.

But that was easier said than done. With the skies darkened by the storm and gusty winds whipping across her face, she was having trouble following the path. What had been, a short while ago, a clearly defined trail was now becoming harder to distinguish.

She kept pushing forward. "Down is good," she said out loud. "Down is good."

They reached a fork in the path. The snow was starting to lay more heavily on the ground. With each step, her boots were sinking deeper into the snow.

She tried to remember which way she'd come up so that she could take the correct path down to the lake. But without the visual references, remembering the right path was not as straightforward as she'd hoped.

A wave of anxiety tore through her. Immediately, her mind went to the worst-case scenario. She imagined the newspaper story: "Foolish woman frozen to death on hike on Christmas Eve. She knew a storm was coming, but she went on a hike anyway!"

The worst part was that she had put Bowzer in danger, a point that the newspaper article would be sure to make. "Also frozen to death by this reckless fool was a wonderful rescue dog named Bowzer. He was an amazing dog, whose joyful energy and friendly disposition will be greatly missed."

Oh, what had she done? She couldn't let anything happen to Bowzer. She had to find a way to safety — a way out of this storm!

Calm yourself, Becca, she told herself. *Take a deep breath.* Her heart, which had been racing with anxiety, started to slow as she forced herself to assess her situation. *Yes, that's good. Now take another breath.*

She could still see the path, despite the wind and snow. Paths were designed to lead somewhere. If she stayed on the path, she'd find her way back home. She could do this. She'd faced adversity before. She could face it again. She took another deep breath.

"We're going to be fine, Bowzer," she said. "We're going to find a way off this mountain and get back home."

Bowzer looked up at her with concern and compassion — smart as he was, he couldn't help but pick up on her fear — and gave her an encouraging bark.

Heart thumping, she led Bowzer on. Oh, she hoped she'd made the right choice at the fork in the path. If she'd picked the wrong path — no, she couldn't think about that.

The storm wasn't going to let up anytime soon, she sensed. And with the afternoon sliding toward dusk, the dim light would soon fade to blackness. And if that happened....

Oh, gosh — she'd forgotten she had her phone with her! She reached into her coat and took it out and pressed the "on" button. Anxiously, she waited for the phone to pick up a signal. *Please please please....*

But no. She wasn't close enough to town. Out here in the wilderness, her phone wasn't going to be any help.

But it would work as a flashlight, she realized. If she was still out here when it got dark, she could use her phone to light the way....

Pushing the thought aside, she turned off her phone and returned it to her coat. She wasn't going to be out here for long, because she was going to find her way back home! She and Bowzer were going to be fine.

With the snow swirling around her and frigid arctic air in her face, she couldn't tell if the path was the same one she had walked up. The trees around her swayed as the wind roared through them.

Suddenly, Bowzer bounded forward. The leash went taut in her hand as he strained toward something that only he could see.

She realized through the gloom that she was walking alongside an open field — and she certainly hadn't passed an open field on her way up the mountain. With a sigh of despair, she realized she'd chosen the wrong path. She'd have to turn around and head back. And with the snow getting thicker by the minute, that wasn't going to be easy.

What had Bowzer seen or smelled that made him suddenly so determined to push forward? Maybe she should trust him and let him take the lead?

Yes, she thought. For a few minutes, at least, she'd let him lead her, rather than the other way around.

"Okay, Bowzer," she said to her canine companion. "What's making you so excited?"

With an eager tug on the leash, Bowzer led her further up the path. And as they reached a bend, she saw why:

Lights!

From a house!

The house was at the top of an open meadow, perhaps a couple hundred yards off the path.

Bowzer could barely restrain himself now. There was a determined eagerness in every ounce of him.

If they went to the house, could she ask for directions? Could she ask to use their phone?

Yes! she nearly said out loud.

The house probably had a driveway. Should she look for the driveway and walk up that? Or should she do what Bowzer clearly wanted her to do — leave the path and bound across the open field of snow?

Bowzer answered that for her. He aimed himself off the path in the direction of the house, pulling her with him.

Amid the howling wind of the storm, she heard a *thwack*. It was a sound she'd heard before but couldn't quite place.

She heard it again, sharp and distinct, and then saw the source.

A man stood in the field, near the house, swinging an ax onto a log, the blade's impact cutting through the storm's roar like a knife through hot butter.

Bowzer barked and rushed forward with so much energy that the leash slipped from her hand.

Before she could say a word, Bowzer blasted through the snowy field and practically leaped at the startled man.

"Bowzer?" she heard the man say, disbelief in his voice. He set down the ax and reached for the dog. He found the leash on Bowzer's collar and said, "What are you doing here?"

Bowzer barked, then turned toward Becca, who was still several yards away, huffing and puffing from running up the hill after Bowzer.

"I'm so sorry!" she said as she approached the man.

"What's going on here?" the man said, disbelief in his voice.

"I'm sorry, I —"

"What do you think you're doing, hiking the trails during a blizzard?" the man said angrily. "Don't you know how dangerous that is?"

CHAPTER 13

*H*e was tall, she realized. Tall and lean, with broad shoulders beneath his mackinaw jacket. He wore a ski cap over brown hair. As she stepped closer, she saw a handsome face with angry brown eyes aimed right at her.

"I'm so sorry," she said. "The weather was so perfect, and the storm came so suddenly —"

"How long have you been out in the storm?" he said, interrupting her.

"For awhile, I guess."

"You need to get inside," he said, in a tone that brooked no debate.

"Are you sure? Maybe if I could use your phone —"

"You and Bowzer need to get out of this storm."

He stepped forward and handed her the

leash, then pointed to the cabin at the top of the hill. "Take him up there." Without another word, he turned and started picking up the wood he'd been chopping.

She blinked at the suddenness of her dismissal. Tears stung her eyes. The man was so angry — and for good reason. She'd put herself and Bowzer in danger. She felt like such a fool.

But his manner toward her — did he have to be so abrupt? Feeling she had no choice, she trudged up the hill toward the cabin, torn between feeling grateful and ashamed and angry.

By the time she and Bowzer reached the cabin's front porch, the man was only a few seconds behind, firewood in his arms. He dropped the firewood onto a stack near the door, then turned to her.

"You sure you're okay?" he asked, giving her and Bowzer another once-over. His voice still had anger in it, but there was concern in his tone as well.

"I'm fine," she said immediately, aware of the defensiveness in her voice and wishing it wasn't there.

The man knelt down and gestured to Bowzer, who instantly went to him and waited patiently while the man gave him a quick examination.

"Good boy," he said, giving Bowzer's ears an affectionate shake.

The man stood and stamped his boots to get the snow off. As he did so, she realized something.

"You know Bowzer," she said. "And he knows you. Why is that?"

He took off his snow cap, revealing a head of shaggy brown hair. He appeared to be a few years older than her — mid-thirties, perhaps. His gaze went from her to Bowzer and back.

"I'm his vet," he said.

"Oh!" she said, with a small gasp of surprise. "You're Dr. Nick."

He gave her a tight smile. "Nick Shepherd, rescuer of lost damsels and dogs, at your service." He stamped his feet one more time, then pushed open the cabin door. "Let's get you and Bowzer inside."

The door swung open, revealing a small, warmly lit mudroom with shoes lined up under a wooden bench and winter coats hanging from hooks on the wood-paneled wall.

The promise of heat inside the cabin drew her closer, like an invisible force field.

"Are you sure?" she said.

"Absolutely. There's no way you can stay outside right now. The storm's only going to get worse."

She stamped her boots to dislodge the snow

and, with Bowzer leading the way, stepped into Dr. Nick's cabin.

Nick followed her in and shut the door behind him. Instantly, the frigid cold disappeared, replaced by a hint of warmth. Her host sat on the bench, untied his boots, then slipped his feet out of them and into a pair of worn moccasins. He stood and shrugged off his mackinaw jacket, revealing a blue wool sweater.

"You can hang your coat on the rack," he said. "Let me get you a pair of slippers." Without another word, he stepped out of the mudroom.

She turned to Bowzer, who was looking up at her with an eager expression. She leaned down and gave him a quick hug. "We'll get home soon, okay? You going to be a good boy as a guest of Dr. Nick?"

Bowzer whined with agreement and waited patiently while she unhooked the leash from his collar. Nose aquiver, he ambled out of the mudroom into the cabin, leaving her to unwrap the scarf from around her neck, take off her gloves, and unzip her heavy winter coat.

Thank goodness she'd decided to dress warmly when she'd left her cottage. If she hadn't.... She shook her head at the thought.

As she was hanging her coat on a hook, Dr. Nick appeared with a pair of fuzzy reindeer slippers. He shrugged apologetically. "These are the only slippers I have that are even close to your size."

She gave him a smile, her first since meeting him. "I'm sure these will be fine, thank you." She took the slippers, sat down on the bench, removed her boots, and stepped into the reindeer slippers. Depending on your point of view, they looked either adorable or silly or both. But at least they were warm and soft.

As she stood up, she realized how incredibly self-conscious she felt. How did her face look after being caught in the storm? And what outfit had she chosen to wear again? A glance down reminded her, to her relief, that she'd picked the burgundy turtleneck sweater and dark ski pants.

She glanced at her host and got the sense that he was feeling awkward as well. He stood there, looking at her, seemingly at a loss for words.

"Please," he finally said, with a welcoming gesture, "come in."

"Thank you," she replied, suddenly overcome by a need to be very polite.

As she stepped from the mudroom, she spied a small mirror on the wall and was gratified by her quick glance: no apparent facial emergencies. A closer inspection would be required, of course, but first she —

Oh, how rude she'd been! She whirled around

and extended her hand. "I haven't introduced myself. Becca Jameson."

Startled by her rapid turnaround, Dr. Nick nearly bumped into her. Recovering, he backed away and blinked, then looked at her offered hand.

"Pleased to meet you," he said. His hand, rough and strong and warm, fit around hers like it was meant to be there. A current passed between them that threatened to take her breath away. She had to restrain herself from gasping.

Quickly, before she made even more of a fool of herself, she removed her hand. He looked up and found herself gazing into a pair of very brown, very surprised eyes.

He blinked again. "Pleased to meet you," he repeated. "I mean, please, come in."

She turned and found herself gazing in appreciation at what she saw. The mudroom led into a beautiful kitchen, spacious and recently renovated, equipped with cherry cabinets, dark-gray marble countertops, and stainless steel appliances. In the center of the kitchen was a large island with a prep sink and a butcher-block countertop. Everything look fresh and crisp and new.

Beyond the kitchen was a wide-open living space designed in the style of a rustic high-end cabin. The walls were made of logs, and wooden beams crisscrossed the cathedral ceiling. Near the kitchen was a dining table with six chairs. A seating area — mocha-colored leather couches and chairs — were in the center of room, facing a roaring fire in a huge stone fireplace.

She leaned against the kitchen island as she took in the warmth and beauty of the space, her fingertips lightly brushing the butcher block countertop. Everything felt so cozy and inviting and comforting. Everything, that is, except her anxiety about why she was here, and the bad opinion that Dr. Nick must have of her.

"You have a beautiful cabin," she said, unable to shake her need to be polite.

"Thank you." After another awkward pause, he added, "Listen, I'm sorry about yelling back there."

She turned to face him. "Oh, no need to apologize—"

"No, I was abrupt." There was something adorable about his awkwardness in that moment. He seemed to be struggling for the right words. "You and Bowzer startled me, but I should have realized that you needed help, not a lecture."

"I totally understand," she said, pleased by his words, but feeling the need to own up to her own mistakes. "And I want to apologize, too! You must have been so surprised to see Bowzer appear from out of nowhere, and in the middle of a storm."

He shrugged and smiled. "Bowzer was about the last thing I expected to see out there."

She smiled back. "He sensed you from quite a ways away. He was practically dragging me toward you."

He glanced across the room to where Bowzer was sniffing near the fireplace before returning to her.

"Well," he said, "I'm glad he did." He paused then, holding her gaze, then said, in a brisker tone, "Now, are you sure you're okay?"

"I'm fine."

"How long were you out in the storm?"

"Not too long. We started our walk a couple of hours ago."

"So not too long. Good. So, no frostbite? No toes or fingers that need warming?"

"I dressed warmly. Luckily for me."

"Good." He blinked suddenly. "I just realized — can I get you something to drink? To eat?"

"Oh, no," she said reflexively. "No, I'm fine."

"You're going to be stuck here awhile," he said, gesturing toward the storm outside. "There's no going out until the blizzard passes. I was planning on hot cocoa when I got done with the firewood. It's no problem at all."

Hot cocoa? She loved hot cocoa. "If you're sure it's no trouble...."

"No trouble at all." He gave her a smile — big

and easy and natural — and turned toward the kitchen. "I'll get Bowzer some food and water, too."

"What can I do to help?"

"Nothing. Make yourself comfortable."

"Would it be okay if I freshen up a bit?" she asked.

"Of course. The bathroom's that way." He pointed across the living room to a hallway that she presumed led to the other rooms in the house.

"Thank you. Be right back."

With a glance at Bowzer, who was now very intently exploring Dr. Nick's dining area, Becca made her way down the hallway. The bathroom was the first door on the left. When she flipped on the light switch, she found herself in a room as new and modern and beautifully decorated as the kitchen, with a new sink, shower/tub, and toilet. The walls were covered with wallpaper — a huge, beautiful, and very dramatic panoramic photo of Heartsprings Valley. She stepped back to look at the photo and realized that the shot had been taken from the same vantage point she'd stood at earlier, while she'd watched the nor'easter sweep across the valley toward her....

She shook herself, grateful that she and Bowzer had found a warm place to ride out the storm, and turned her attention to her real goal: the mirror. It had been a couple of hours since she'd checked her face at the cottage, and a lot had happened to it since then, including a raging storm!

As she examined herself in the mirror, she realized she'd been lucky. No makeup disasters had occurred. In fact, looking at her reflection, she would hardly have guessed that, mere minutes ago, she'd been lost on a mountain in a wet wintry mess.

There was something so surreal about her situation. How could Heartsprings Valley, a gentle town populated with some of the nicest people she'd ever met, be the cause of so much craziness? Because — and there was no doubt about this — the past two days had been crazy! In the past twenty-four hours, she'd experienced all manner of the unexpected: A new canine companion. Caught in a dangerous winter storm. In the cabin of a stranger. A stranger who seemed very attractive, by the way. A stranger who also, once he got over his initial anger and shock of their initial meeting, seemed decent and nice....

She felt a stab of excitement mixed with guilt as she realized where her thoughts were heading. Yes, she forced herself to acknowledge, she'd felt an attraction to this man. The electricity that passed between them when he took her hand in his — that had been real. She took a deep breath.

Tears threatened. She took another deep breath to push them down.

You're making more of this than you need to and certainly much more than you should, she told herself. *Calm down, girl.*

The feeling she thought of as attraction — she was probably mistaken. What she was feeling was *gratitude* to Dr. Nick for helping her and Bowzer and offering them shelter from the storm. He was just being decent and neighborly. He was Bowzer's vet. That's what his friendliness was about.

There's nothing more to it than that. She and Dr. Nick were new neighbors, that was all. She would see him from time to time around town. They would chat. Maybe over time they would become friends. That happened sometimes, right?

And about finding him attractive — well, so what? The world was full of men who were tall and handsome, with broad shoulders and warm brown eyes. No doubt she would find those men attractive, too. She was human, after all. Was there any harm in noticing a fine-looking fellow every now and then?

She took another deep breath and exhaled, then breathed in and out again, relieved to feel herself calming down. It was good to check in with herself occasionally. She liked herself better when her head was in the right emotional space.

Idly, she twisted the ring on the third finger of her left hand. She opened her mouth wide to make sure her teeth were still clean — always an important precaution! — and gave herself a test smile.

Squaring her shoulders, she turned, opened the bathroom door, and headed back to the kitchen.

CHAPTER 14

The first thing Becca encountered was — a standoff!

In the center of the room, a regal white cat was holding court from the dining room table, gazing with aloof disdain at a very curious and very intimidated Bowzer, who was down on his haunches and inching forward, as if approaching royalty.

The cat turned and surveyed Becca with cool grey eyes.

"Oh my," Becca said as she got closer. "Who do we have here?"

"Meet Divina," Nick said as he took a carton of milk from the refrigerator. "The undisputed queen of the castle."

"She's beautiful," Becca said, admiring the cat's lovely white coat.

"Thirteen years old and going strong," Nick said.

"Is it okay if I...?"

"You can try. She's a bit .... choosy. Don't take it personally if she doesn't warm up to you right away."

Becca slowly approached the regal cat, who watched her approach with mild interest.

"Hello, Divina," she said as she held out her hand. "My name is Becca."

Divina graciously deigned to give Becca's hand an exploratory sniff, then consented to have her ears stroked.

Becca pulled out a dining chair and sat down next to Divina. "Come here, girl," she said, gesturing toward her lap.

Divina gazed at Becca for a few seconds, still as a statue. Then, with a smooth sinuous flow, she rose, stretched her back, and dropped with dainty paws from the table onto Becca's knees.

"Aww..." Becca said. "You are such a sweetheart." She reached out and gently stroked Divina's soft fur as the queen of the cabin leaned in closer and sniffed Becca's face.

And then — the queen purred.

"Wow," Nick said.

Becca looked up and saw that Nick was watching them, fascinated.

"She's very picky."

Divina purred again, then settled herself onto Becca's lap.

"She's such a darling," Becca said, her attention returning to the ball of fur on her lap, glowing with pleasure as the cat relaxed and purred again.

Nick cleared his throat. "You're the first person since...."

His voice trailed off. When he didn't finish his sentence, Becca looked up and saw the same confused look on his face that she'd seen when they shook hands.

"Sorry," he said, "where was I?" He took a deep breath and clapped his hands together. "Hot cocoa."

Becca smiled. "Is there anything I can do to help?"

"Not until Divina decides to let you," he said, turning back to the refrigerator. "From the look of things, that might be awhile."

On the floor next to her chair, Bowzer was continuing to inch closer, intensely curious about the cat but also clearly aware that the queen of the cabin required careful handling.

"Do you want to meet Divina?" Becca said to him.

With a whine of anticipation, Bowzer rose and slowly approached Becca's knee, his nose quivering with excitement.

Divina, lolling about in contented splendor in Becca's lap, stretched her legs and continued to act like the approaching dog didn't exist. She purred again and, still utterly relaxed, shifted onto her side to face Bowzer.

Bowzer whimpered softly, eagerness in every quiver. His nose got closer and closer and —

Divina's paw whipped out and smacked his sensitive snout!

CHAPTER 15

*W*ith a surprised yelp, Bowzer backed off.

Becca and Nick couldn't help themselves — they both laughed!

"Oh, you poor thing," Becca said, laughing some more as Bowzer looked at Divina, perplexed. "Are you okay?"

"He's fine," Nick said. "Hey, Bowzer, you want some food?"

At the sound of his name and the word "food," Bowzer's head whipped around. Whatever pain or confusion he was feeling instantly vanished. With a happy wag of his tail, he ran into the kitchen.

Nick bent down to give him a hug. "If I remember right, big fellah, you like a mix of wet and crunchy."

With a joyful bark, Bowzer followed Nick into the mudroom.

Becca watched from her chair at the dining room table, unable to move without dislodging the queen. In her lap, Divina rolled over again, this time looking straight up, surveying Becca with approval.

"You are such a beautiful cat," Becca cooed. "Such soft fur. Don't tell Bowzer, but I love your attitude." She giggled. "But go easy on the poor guy, okay? He's actually a sweetheart. I think you and he could become great friends."

Divina purred softly in response, as if giving Becca's plea thoughtful consideration.

From the mudroom, Becca heard the sounds of a cabinet opening and dry dog food being poured into a dog dish. She heard Bowzer give a satisfied yelp. Nick popped into the kitchen with a water bowl, which he rinsed in the sink. He filled it, then brought it back to the mudroom.

A minute later, he stepped back into the kitchen. "Now," he said, rubbing his hands together, "where were we? That's right, cocoa."

Divina chose that moment to rise to her feet. She purred again, leaned closer to rub her nose against Becca's cheek to thank her for the use of her lap, then smoothly dropped to the floor.

"Divina's done with my lap," she said.

Nick smiled, then reached into a spice cabinet to take out more ingredients.

Becca stood and joined him in the kitchen. "I feel like I need to have something to do. Please, let me help."

"Okay, I'm getting the ingredients ready." He pointed to a recipe on an index card on the counter. "Can you doublecheck to make sure I have everything?"

She picked up the recipe and saw the title: "Grandma's Secret Cocoa." She smiled. "Your grandma?"

Nick nodded. "Every Christmas, she made it for us. A Shepherd family tradition. For years, we never knew the recipe. She kept it secret. Every year, we begged and begged. Finally, about a year before she passed on, she gave a copy of the recipe to each of her grandkids. Every time I have some of her cocoa, I feel like she's here with me."

Becca felt an emotional tug at his words, spoken so clearly and simply. "I feel the same way about gingerbread."

"Gingerbread? Why's that?"

"I made my very first gingerbread house with the help of my mom and grandma. I was eight years old."

"A home builder from an early age?"

"My mom took pictures of my first house," she said with a smile. "Frankly, it was a total mess.

The walls didn't stand up straight, the windows were oddly shaped, and the roof had a big gap at the top."

"Not up to today's exacting construction standards?" Nick said with a grin.

"Oh, gosh, no," she said with a laugh. "The poor house would have blown down at the slightest breeze. But I was very proud of myself. My construction techniques have definitely improved over time."

"I wish I could say the same about my cocoa-making skills." He looked at the ingredients he'd lined up on the counter, a frown on his face. "I think this is right, but...."

Becca's gaze returned to the recipe in her hand, then scanned the ingredients on the counter.

"Looks like you've got it. Milk, cocoa powder, vanilla extract, sugar, salt, cinnamon...." She paused and picked up a container. "Chili powder?"

"Essential," he said with a vigorous nod. "Just enough to rev the chocolate into high gear."

She didn't know what to say about that — his description seemed more *automotive* than culinary — but she kept her opinion to herself.

"For the whipped cream," she said, "it's best to start with a chilled bowl and whisk."

"I put the bowl and whisk in the freezer a few minutes ago," he said with a grin.

"Excellent," she said, then pointed to the recipe. "The only ingredient I don't see is nutmeg."

"Ah, good catch."

He brushed past her as he reached into a small basket on the counter and plucked out an actual nutmeg.

"Here we go. We grate it to get some flecks onto the whipped cream, just before we drink it."

With him so close, she was reminded again how tall he was, and how perfectly his sweater fit his broad shoulders. She sensed his body heat, and was suddenly very aware of her own body responding. Without warning and much to her chagrin, her cheeks flushed.

Fortunately, nutmeg now in hand, Nick chose that moment to step back to where he'd been, restoring the four-foot buffer that felt infinitely more comfortable.

"Are you feeling okay?" he said, noticing her flushed cheeks.

"Fine, totally fine," she said quickly — too quickly? Desperately, she turned her attention to the nutmeg. "So, about the nutmeg," she said, aware even as she said that she didn't care a whit about nutmeg. "That's quite an ingredient."

Quite an ingredient? She couldn't believe herself. She wanted to scream.

Nick didn't notice. Or maybe he noticed but pretended not to. He nodded and casually tossed the nutmeg in his hand. "Yep," he said, "it's the final touch." She noticed that his hand, the one doing the tossing, was a strong and well-made hand. A hand that took care of all manner of creatures. It was, indeed, a very good hand.

A very good hand? What was she thinking?

"So," she said, "let's get started." *Please!*

"Right." He opened one of the lower cabinet drawers and pulled out a saucepan to heat the milk, then set it down on the counter.

"Enough for ... two helpings each?" he asked.

"Sure," she said as she watched him pour milk into the saucepan.

"Low heat, right?" he said as he placed the saucepan on a burner on the stove.

"That's right, not too hot. We want the milk to warm gradually."

He turned on the gas heater. With a gentle whoosh, a blue flame ignited. He dialed it back a notch. "That look okay?"

"Perfect."

"It'll take a couple of minutes to warm. So tell me about you and Bowzer. How are the two of you doing?"

"Oh, he's wonderful," Becca said. "Even

though it's been just a day, already I can't imagine life without him." She paused. "You weren't at the clinic yesterday when I met him. Did Dr. Gail tell you?"

He nodded. "She called and told me last night. She said the new town librarian and Bowzer had fallen for each other. 'Love at first sight,' she said."

Becca laughed. "Was I that obvious?"

"Apparently so." At that moment, Bowzer ambled back from the mudroom and made straight for Nick.

Nick reached down and gave him a hug. "This guy and I are buds. Aren't we, Bowzer?"

Bowzer barked in agreement, delighted by the attention.

"I promised him we'd find him a good home," Nick said, glancing up from Bowzer to Becca.

She felt it then — the responsibility of her decision. But with that feeling came another feeling — a feeling of happiness that she'd made the leap.

"I promise he'll have a wonderful home with me," she said.

Nick nodded, his brown eyes gazing at her with approval. "I know he will — I can tell."

On the stove, the blue flame of the burner was doing its work. Nick gave the milk a stir. "What do you think?"

She leaned closer. "It's warming up nicely."

"Time to add the sugar and cocoa?"

She nodded. He opened a drawer stuffed with cooking utensils and took out measuring cups and spoons. Glancing at the recipe for confirmation, he opened the sugar container and scooped out the right amount.

Becca reached into the utensils drawer and picked out a stirring spoon. "I'll stir while you add the ingredients."

"Sounds good." Slowly, he added the sugar and followed with the cocoa while Becca swirled the spoon through the warm milk. Conscious of his proximity, she kept her attention fixed firmly on the saucepan. Now that she knew she was prone to responding unconsciously to his physical presence, she could take steps to prevent herself from falling into more of the silliness of a few minutes before.

You're making hot cocoa, that's it, she reminded herself. *With a stranger. A friendly stranger, but a stranger nonetheless.*

"We keep stirring the pot until the sugar and cocoa are dissolved, right?" he said.

"Exactly." She sensed his focus on her. How she knew that she couldn't tell — she was keeping her own eyes glued to the saucepan, thank you very much — but somehow she felt it. There was some invisible force, some unseen connection, reaching across the small distance that separated them.

She resisted the impulse to look up. Her fingers gripped the stirring spoon more tightly. The delightful aroma of cocoa and warm milk tickled her nose.

"What's next?" she said briskly.

"When the sugar and cocoa are dissolved, we add the other ingredients. We stir the pot for a few more minutes, then make the whipped cream. Then we pour the cocoa into the mugs, add the whipped cream, and sprinkle on the nutmeg."

"The stirring's going well — the last of the cocoa is dissolving now."

"Goo. It's been awhile since I made Grandma's cocoa — I'd forgotten how much I enjoy it."

"I think it's ready."

With an eye on the recipe, he used measuring spoons to add the remaining ingredients. The cocoa was becoming toasty now, with waves of heat shimmering over the surface.

"You okay with the stirring while I make the whipped cream?" he asked.

"More than okay," she said as she leaned in for a whiff of pure chocolate loveliness. "I could stand here and inhale this wonderful smell all night."

He opened the freezer and took out the chilled

bowl and whisk, then grabbed a small carton of heavy cream from the fridge. She watched him pour the cream into the bowl and begin whipping it by hand, putting real energy and concentration into the task. She'd always relied on an electric mixer — the old-fashioned way looked so hard! — but she found herself feeling glad that Nick was putting muscle into it.

"I can tell you've done this before," she said as he moved the whisk rapidly through the heavy cream.

"Only when I make Grandma's cocoa," he said. After another minute or so, when the cream looked almost ready to peak, he put the whisk down, grabbed a box of confectioner's sugar from a cabinet and, using just his eyes to measure, sprinkled in the appropriate amount. He whipped the cream for a few seconds more to help the sugar dissolve, then turned around and picked up vanilla extract on the counter and added that. A few more twists of the whisk and the whipped cream was ready, its peaks rising firmly and temptingly into the air.

"Okay, not just for cocoa," he said, giving her a grin. "Also for my mom's cherry pie."

"Aha," Becca said. "A pie lover!"

"Big-time," he said with a grin.

"Your timing couldn't be better." She eyed the saucepan. "The cocoa is ready."

"Excellent." He opened an upper cabinet and took out two mugs. One mug, big and red and stocky, had the name of his vet clinic on it. The other, creamy white and much more elegant, had a lovely curved shape.

"That's a beautiful piece," she said, nodding toward the white mug.

"Thanks." He rinsed the two mugs in the sink, then took a folded dish towel from a kitchen drawer and dried them carefully, set them on the counter next to the stove, and turned off the burner. "Would you like me to pour?"

"Please." She stepped back, her sense of antici-pation climbing ever-higher as the heat and aroma of the hot cocoa stirred her senses.

He slipped on an oven mitt, picked up the saucepan, and skillfully poured hot cocoa into both mugs. He set the saucepan on a burner and set it to lowest heat. "More for later."

"I'll add the whipped cream."

"Go for it." Using a spoon, she scooped a healthy dollop of cream into each mug, then plopped the spoon in her mouth to enjoy the sweet coolness of the freshly whipped cream.

He opened his utensil drawer and rummaged around until he found a microplane grater. He picked up the nutmeg and, with a look of concen-tration, ran the grater over the nutmeg, sprin-kling flecks over each mug.

Her stomach growled as the wonderful mix of aromas filled her lungs. With a start, she realized she hadn't eaten anything since wolfing down that poor gingerbread cookie before leaving the cottage.

Nick picked up the white mug, now nearly overflowing with cocoa goodness, and handed it to Becca. As her hand closed over the mug, her fingers brushed his hand, sending another jolt through her.

The mug was so warm in her hand. She leaned in and breathed in the heavenly aroma, the nutmeg enhancing the cocoa wonderfully.

Nick picked up his red mug and held it in front of him.

"A toast," he said.

She straightened and raised her mug in front of her.

"To Bowzer," he said, "who made this moment possible."

Becca smiled and glanced toward Bowzer, who'd heard his name and was looking expectantly at the two of them.

"And to your grandmother," Becca said. "May her recipe and spirit live on."

"Amen."

CHAPTER 16

*T*hey sipped from the cups then, and Becca's immediate thought was: *Oh my.* The cocoa was fantastic, the sensations rolling through her mouth. So creamy and rich and chocolaty. So smooth. So *luxurious*. The chili in the recipe crept up on her, sneaking into her awareness in a refreshing and subtle way, adding the pleasing kick that Nick had talked about.

Moments like this, Becca decided as she reveled in the cocoa's comforting goodness, were what life was about.

Nick closed his eyes as he took his first sip. She used the opportunity to really examine his face. His thick brown hair was a touch too unruly, perhaps, and in need of a trim. His eyelashes looked fuller than hers, she noted enviously. His straight nose and strong jaw were like something out a magazine ad. He hadn't shaved that day, her gaze lingering on his dark stubble. His skin would feel rough if she ran her hand over it —

Wait. Why was she thinking that? *Stop it!* she told herself.

He opened his eyes then, and she found herself staring into their dark brown depths.

"Good stuff," he said.

He was talking about the cocoa, of course. And it was good. It was very good. It was —

"Delicious," she said. "So delicious."

"Why don't we sit down?" He gestured toward the living room.

"Sounds great," she said, exhaling with relief. He led the way and she followed to the leather sofa near the fire. He settled on one end, and she was about to join him when her attention was drawn to a set of photographs on the fireplace mantel.

"May I?" she asked, gesturing toward the photos.

"Please."

She stepped closer. The photos were clearly of Nick's family. Nick with his mother and father and —

"Your brother and sister?" she said, pointing to a photo.

He nodded. "I'm the youngest of three."

"Do they live here in Heartsprings Valley?"

He shook his head. "No, I'm a transplant here. Like you."

Her gaze landed then on a photo of Nick with his arms around a young woman. She and Nick were both laughing, her brown hair flowing over her shoulders.

"This must be your wife," she said.

"That's right," he said quietly.

"Abby told me she died in a car crash two years ago. I'm so sorry for your loss."

"I miss her every day," he said. "It's been two years, but sometimes it feels like it was yesterday."

She nodded, then joined him on the couch and turned to face him. The mug in her hands offered comfort, its warmth a reassuring presence. "I lost my husband three years ago."

His brown eyes widened with compassion. "I'm so sorry to hear that. Can I ask what happened?"

She took a deep breath. "He was in Afghanistan, on his second deployment there. A landmine. I'm told he died instantly."

He shook his head. "I'm so sorry for your loss."

Her lower lip quivered. "One minute you have your whole life ahead of you, and the next...."

He swallowed. "Suddenly, everything is gone."

They sat in silence for a long moment and allowed the quiet to linger. In front of them, the fire burned steadily, casting flickering lights. For the first time since setting foot in the cabin, she felt at peace. The awkwardness she'd felt, the self-consciousness, the fear and anxiety — all of that had vanished. She and Nick had found common ground, a bridge, a connection. Both of them, it turned out, were lost souls, adrift, unsure how to find their way forward from what had been ripped from them.

"Was your wife the reason you moved to Heartsprings Valley?" she said.

He nodded. "Her idea. She'd spent a summer here as a kid, and the town had captured her imagination and never really let go. I wasn't sure, but I talked with the vet here — Gail's previous vet partner — and he was getting ready to retire and he encouraged us to give it a try and introduced me and Gail. He told me I'd never get bored up here, and boy, was he right about that."

She smiled. "I've only been here three days, but I have to agree. This town is full of surprises."

"It's a whirlwind sometimes. So much happening, usually all at once."

"Abby said you take care of all kinds of animals, even iguanas?"

"Sure," he said with a smile. "They're actually kind of cute, in baby-Godzilla kind of way."

"I saw a picture of Pinkie the pig on the wall in the waiting room. He looks adorable."

He chuckled. "A very determined fellow. Smart as all get-out, too."

"Did Dr. Gail say something about a sick llama? Am I remembering that right?"

"You mean Daisy. Angus has a farm about a mile outside of town and raises llamas. One of his gals — her name's Daisy — is having a difficult pregnancy, so we're keeping an eye on her."

He shifted position on the sofa and took another sip of his cocoa. "So what brought you here?"

She took a deep breath and exhaled. "Well, the easy answer is that I applied for the town librarian job and got hired, so here I am. But there's more to it than that. After my husband died, I survived by going on auto-pilot. I went through the motions, but I felt like I was numb all over, like I no longer cared, like I couldn't *risk* caring. I threw myself into my job — I worked in a library — and buried myself in my work."

He nodded at that, clearly relating, encouraging her to continue.

"Looking back, I think I *needed* to be busy and numbed-out," she said. "For me, that's how I coped. If I hadn't had my job, I don't know what I would have done."

"Same with me. The busier I am, the less time I have to be reminded of...."

"Exactly. But earlier this year, I felt a shift inside. I felt ... I don't know how to describe this, but I felt *stale*. Like I was numbed out not because I still *needed* to be, but because I was in the *habit* of being that way."

He blinked, surprised. "I've never thought of it that way, but I see what you mean."

"On the same day I realized that, I saw the job listing for the librarian position in Heartsprings Valley. On an impulse, I updated my resume and applied. Never in a million years did I think I'd be considered seriously — I probably wouldn't have applied if I had! — but Hettie Mae reached out and one thing led to another and here I am."

"Any regrets?"

"No," she said with a decisive shake of her head. "I've met such good people here. Hettie Mae, of course, but also Abby from the chocolate shop and Dr. Gail and Bert Winters and now you." She gestured toward Bowzer, who was dozing quietly on the rug in front of the fire. "And of course this guy here."

She paused as she realized something. "Although, I do have one regret about moving here when I did."

"What's that?"

"Christmas is such a special time for my family — my mom and dad, my two younger brothers and their families — and being here means I'm not celebrating with them."

"Is there a reason you moved here before Christmas?"

"I could have waited until after the holiday," she said. "Part of me wishes I'd done that. The thought of being with my mom right now in her kitchen, helping her making her famous apple pie...." She sighed wistfully, imagining her mom's laughter and the wonderful aromas of pie dough and cinnamon and freshly sliced apples.

"But I couldn't," she said, sitting up straighter. "Somehow, I knew that my fresh start in Heartsprings Valley had to begin right away. It's like I was ... pulled here."

He gazed upon her intently, focused on her every word. "I think I can guess why," he said.

"Really? Because I'm still not sure about that myself."

CHAPTER 17

*N*ick took a deep breath. "Well....
Going out on a limb here.... I think
you had to get here before Christmas because you
needed to break free from the Christmas you
know and love at home, because those traditions
you know and love so much intensify the pain
you feel about the loss of your husband. Plain
and simple, you needed a fresh start, including a
fresh start for Christmas."

It was like he had seen into her soul — like he
understood instantly how torn up she was by her
decision, how much she regretted it but at the
same time needed it.

And she realized something about him in that
instant — something that had registered in her
subconscious as soon as she'd set foot in his

cabin, but which hadn't pushed its way to the front of her mind until this moment. Here they were, in a beautiful rustic cabin on a snowy mountain on Christmas Eve, but not a single holiday decoration was in sight. No Christmas tree, no wreaths, no holly, no ornaments, no Christmas cards on the mantel — nothing.

"You have the same need, don't you?" she said. "That's why you've banished Christmas."

He blinked then, like he was holding back a surge of emotion. "I used to love Christmas," he said, "but it became too painful, so I quit it."

"Christmas never quits on you. It's always there, ready to welcome you back."

He swallowed, then took a deep breath. "I don't know if I'm ready for that."

She had an insight then about something else. "I got a call this morning from Dr. Gail, inviting me to come by the clinic tomorrow afternoon for a Christmas Day gathering. She organized that gathering for you, didn't she?"

He sighed. "She's a good friend."

"Are you going?"

"I don't know. She did the same thing last year, but I begged off."

"Well," she said, "like you said, we all have our own way of coping. You'll know when it's time to let Christmas back into your life."

He gave her a slow smile. "You're not going to get on my case about it?"

"Nope," she said firmly. "A man's gotta do what a man's gotta do." Then she added, "Or woman, as the case may be."

His eyebrows furrowed. "Sounds like a certain woman had to do what she had to do? Is there a story there?"

She sighed. "I lied to my mom. I told her my new job started the week before Christmas. I feel terrible about that."

"Well, don't beat yourself up too much. Someday soon, you'll fess up and she'll be mad at you, but eventually she'll understand."

"How can you know that?"

"Because anyone who makes apple pie that's good enough to be famous has to be a generous, forgiving person. Everyone knows the key ingredient to great apple pie is love."

She smiled at that. "Her apple pie is amazing."

"She sounds like an amazing mom."

"She is." With a start, she remembered that she and her mom hadn't talked since that morning. "Would it be okay if I gave her a call?"

"Sure," he said.

She got up from the couch and he followed.

"Would you like more cocoa?" he said.

"Thank you. That would be lovely." She finished off the last swallow and handed him her mug. With a smile, he gestured for her lead the way, so she walked across the living room and through the kitchen into the mudroom, where she reached into her coat pocket and pulled out her phone. She turned it on and looked at it and frowned.

"My phone isn't picking up a signal," she said.

From the kitchen, Nick said, "Service out here is spotty at best. And the storm isn't helping. I have a landline. You're welcome to use it."

"Are you sure?"

"Of course. The phone's next to the couch in the living room."

"Thank you." She put her phone back in her coat pocket, then returned to the living room, picked up the phone, and punched in the number she knew by heart.

On the second ring, the phone picked up and she heard her mom say, "Hello?"

"Hi, Mom, it's me."

"Becca? You're calling from a new number. Is this the number for your new house?"

"No, Mom, I'm calling from a ... friend's house." The thought came then: Were she and Nick friends? Did they know each other well enough to call each other that?

"A friend? Who's that?" her mom asked.

"His name is Nick. Nick Shepherd. He's Bowzer's veterinarian."

"Well, that's nice. Is he having a Christmas Eve gathering? Why are you using his phone and not yours?"

"He lives outside of town, so cell service is spotty, especially with the storm."

"The storm? What storm?"

"A snowstorm. It's called a nor'easter."

"Oh, Becca, that doesn't sound good." She heard her mother say to someone: "It's Becca. There's a snowstorm there! A *nor'easter*."

"Mom, I'm fine. Bowzer and I are here at Dr. Nick's cabin."

"Well, how did you get there in the storm?"

Oh, boy. "Bowzer and I were on a hike when the storm hit."

"You were *outside* when the nor'easter hit?" her mother said, her voice rising in anxiety.

"Mom, we're fine."

"What were you doing outside on a hike? It's cold up there. You could get frostbite."

"I promise, Mom, I'm fine and Bowzer's fine. Dr. Nick has been a wonderful host."

"I want to speak with him."

"What? No, Mom."

"Yes. Right now, young lady."

Becca bit her lip. She could argue, but what good would that do? She knew how determined her mom could be. And she knew that Nick, mere feet away in the kitchen, could hear her every word.

She sighed. "Okay, just a minute."

Holding her hand over the phone's receiver, she said, "Guess what? My mom wants to talk to you."

Nick turned from the stove, surprised. "Me?"

"She wants to make sure the storm didn't turn me into a popsicle."

He smiled and held up the stirring spoon. "We'll switch. You stir, I'll talk."

She put the phone down, stepped into the kitchen, and took the spoon from him. The lovely aroma of cocoa and milk and spices wafted up from the saucepan.

Nick walked into the living room and picked up the phone.

"Hi, this is Nick," he said, then listened.

After a moment he said, "Yes, ma'am. She and Bowzer are both fine."

He listened some more, then said, "No, it's not a problem at all, ma'am." Following that, he listened and then said, "Yes, ma'am" three more times. Each time he spoke, Becca felt her anxiety rise. What was her mother saying?

Finally, with a smile on his face, Nick gestured to Becca to come to the phone. "And very nice talking with *you*, ma'am," he said. Becca rushed into the living room and took the phone from an amused Nick, who went back to the kitchen for more cocoa-stirring duty.

Becca took a breath to calm herself, then brought the phone to her mouth. "I'm back, Mom. Did you and Nick have a nice chat?"

"He seems like a very nice man," her mom said.

"He is."

"It was very kind of him to offer you shelter from the storm."

"Very kind."

"Are you okay up there? You know I worry about you."

"I'm fine, Mom. I promise."

She heard her mother sigh, and knew from that sigh that her mom was starting to calm down.

"I wish you could be here," her mom said.

"I know. Me, too."

"Hold on, dear. Your father just Googled him."

"He did *what*?"

"Oh, my," her mom said, clearly distracted by what her father had found on the computer. "He's very handsome. Is he single?"

"Mother!"

"Now, don't jump all over me. You know I want what's best for you."

Becca gritted her teeth. "We can talk about this *later*."

"Okay, I can take a hint. You call me when you can, okay?"

"I'll call you tomorrow morning."

"Merry Christmas, dear. Love you!"

"Merry Christmas, mom! Love you too!"

CHAPTER 18

*B*ecca placed the receiver back in the cradle and turned toward Nick, who looked amused.

"Sorry about that," she said. "When my mom gets protective, she gets *very* protective."

"She sounds like a wonderful mom," Nick said.

"She's the best," Becca said as she joined him in the kitchen. She watched him turn the burner off, pick up the saucepan, and carefully pour cocoa into their mugs.

Unable to stop herself, she asked, "What did she say to you?"

"She asked if you were okay after being out in the storm. She asked if it was okay for you to stay here during the storm. And then she basically asked more variations of the same two questions."

"I'm sorry you had to do that," she said.

"No problem," he said with a grin. "Your mom's worried about you, that's all."

They worked together wordlessly to get their second round of cocoa ready. The tentativeness from earlier was gone, replaced by an instinctive sense of what they expected from each other. As the whipped cream got dolloped and the nutmeg got sprinkled, Becca felt like she was in a flow of movement and purpose that seemed designed for the two of them. When Nick handed over her mug, she sensed that maybe, must maybe, he was feeling the same thing.

Silently, they made their way to the couch. Becca breathed in the wonderful aroma of the cocoa and licked the whipped cream on the top. A dash of nutmeg tingled on her tongue.

Bowzer was still dozing in front of the fire, his breathing regular and relaxed.

Nick cleared his throat. "I try not to get overly attached to the animals in my care, but with Bowzer, I couldn't help myself. He's a very special dog."

"I sensed that from the instant I saw him," she said.

At that moment, the queen of the cabin chose to grace them with an appearance, making her way down the hallway into the living room. She surveyed Nick and Becca on the couch with silent approval, then regarded Bowzer silently, as if making up her mind about something.

"Uh-oh," Becca said with a smile.

Slowly, Divina approached the sleeping dog, pausing several times to sniff cautiously before stepping closer.

"What do think she's going to do?" Becca whispered.

"I have no idea," Nick whispered back.

Divina stopped in front of Bowzer's face. Was she going to whack him on the nose again? Becca bit her lip, restraining an urge to warn her dog of the impending danger.

But no. Divina stretched her back, then moved closer to the oblivious canine. For several long seconds, she contemplated his sleeping form. Finally, as if settling on an important decision, she did something that made both Becca and Nick gasp:

She lay down next to Bowzer and snuggled into his chest!

"Well, I'll be," Nick said, his eyes wide and disbelieving.

"Oh. My. Gosh," Becca whispered.

Awakened by Divina's divine presence, Bowzer looked up and discovered the queen of the cabin nestled next to him. He blinked but remained perfectly still except for his tail, which thumped happily. Divina glanced up at Bowzer's face, then settled closer to her new friend and promptly went to sleep.

Bowzer looked up at Nick and Becca, surprise and happiness radiating from him, then turned his gaze toward the sleeping queen of the cabin. Settling his head down, he followed Divina into contented slumber.

Nick chuckled softly, then turned toward Becca. "We'll have to make sure these two new friends spend lots of time together."

"Of course," Becca said, then blinked when she realized what that meant. It meant that she and Nick would also have to spend time together. Which meant — what? From the way her heart suddenly thumped in her chest, the answer to that question had, without warning, become extremely important. She felt her breathing constrict as she realized that her interest in spending time with Nick could mean only one thing. It meant that —

Her thoughts were interrupted by an unfamiliar crackling noise, from somewhere down the hallway. The sound was like a speakerphone connected to a static-filled line. She heard a man's voice say, "Dr. Nick, you out there? Over."

"What's that?" she asked.

"CB radio," Nick said. He rose and stepped

out of the living room. Unable to restrain herself, Becca followed him down the hallway into a room set up as an office. On a desk stood a CB radio.

Nick picked up the receiver. "Nick here. Angus, that you? Over."

"Doc, it's Daisy," Angus said, his voice crackling through the radio. "Looks like it's time."

"Anything showing?"

"One leg."

"Just one?"

"Just one."

Nick's mouth tightened. "You keep her calm. I'll be there in forty-five. Over."

"Thanks, doc." Even through the static, the relief in Angus's voice was crystal-clear. "See you soon. Over."

CHAPTER 19

*N*ick stood still for a few seconds, frowning. Then he put the receiver back in the cradle and turned. He blinked when he realized Becca was in the study with him.

"Sorry," he said, startled.

"Is everything okay?" she asked.

He shook his head. "That was Angus. He's the llama farmer I talked about. One of his gals — Daisy — is due and her pregnancy hasn't been easy. Now her cria — baby — is coming out the wrong way."

"Wrong way? How so?"

He nodded. "From the sound of it, one of the cria's feet is positioned the wrong way. The condition she's in is dangerous. I need to get out there."

"What can I do to help?"

He took a deep breath. "I'm really sorry about all this. I was looking forward to a quiet evening in front of the fire. I'm ... enjoying getting to know you." The same awkwardness from earlier had returned. "You and Bowzer should make yourselves comfortable. I'm not sure how long I'll be gone."

He stepped past her. "Excuse me. I need to get changed."

She heard his bedroom door close. She stood in the study for a few seconds, adjusting herself to this new situation, then walked back into the living room. Bowzer, still wrapped around Divina, looked up with curiosity but didn't budge from his spot. Clearly, he understand how essential it was for him to continue to be Divina's canine pillow.

She stepped to a window and looked into the blackness of the night. Outside, the storm was going strong. Through the cabin's thick walls, she heard the faint roar of the wind as it whipped through the trees and swirled snow through the air. The blanket of white on the ground looked like it was getting thicker by the second. She wondered how long the storm would be with them before moving on.

Safe and snug in Nick's cabin, she looked at her sleeping dog and his new feline friend in front of the crackling fireplace and felt a surge of gratitude for everything that had happened to her since she'd moved to Heartsprings Valley. Christmas was still hours away, but already she knew that this holiday would be one of her most unusual and memorable ever.

Nick walked back into the living room. He'd changed into heavy winter overalls and thrown a second sweater over his red one.

"I have meats and cheeses and veggies in the fridge," he said as he stepped into the kitchen, "and a loaf of bread on the counter. Also, there's soup in the pantry. Please feel free to have any or all of it. Also, there's food for Bowzer in the mudroom."

She nodded, and was about to thank him when she realized something. "Nick, I —"

"I don't know how long I'll be," he said as he pulled out a medical kit from the pantry. "But I might be gone all night. The guest room is ready, and there are towels in the linen closet in the hall if you want to take a shower."

"Nick, I —"

"I'm sorry I have to head out like this," he said, looking around to make sure he had what he needed. "But duty calls."

"Nick," she said again.

"I —"

"Nick."

He stopped, then went still, finally giving her his full attention.

The words came out of her mouth before she even knew what she was going to say.

"Nick," she said, "I'm going with you."

CHAPTER 20

*N*ick blinked with surprise. "No," he said immediately. "You should stay here."

"I'm going," she said. "I want to help."

"The storm isn't done with us."

"Bowzer and Divina will keep each other company, and I'll come along to help you out."

"It would be safer —"

"You do have a passenger seat, right?"

"Yes," he said, "but —"

"Then it's settled," she said brightly.

"It's not what you think. And in this storm —"

"Nonsense," she said. "I'll be fine."

Without waiting for him to respond, she stepped into the mudroom and began putting on her boots.

He followed and watched her for a few

seconds. "I'm pretty sure my passenger seat isn't what you're expecting."

"I'll be fine," she said confidently, though a voice inside her chose that moment to pipe up and whisper, *Girl, what are you doing?*

She stood up, took her heavy winter coat from the rack, and shrugged herself into it.

Nick frowned as he watched her button herself up. He seemed to be weighing what to say or do next.

She picked up her scarf, wrapped it snugly around her throat, and slipped into her gloves.

"Okay, I'm ready." When he didn't respond, she added, as much for herself as for him, "Listen, I really want to do this. I know there must be something I can do to help. I don't like the thought of you being out all night by yourself. I'd feel terrible if I was stuck here, enjoying your hospitality in your cabin, knowing that you're out there in the cold."

He almost said no — she could tell by the flash of his brown eyes — but then he sighed. "Okay, fine, you can come. But you're free to change your mind when you see what you're in for."

"Let's get going."

He turned and said, "Bowzer!"

Within seconds, the dog joined them in the mudroom.

Nick gestured toward the leash, hanging on the rack. "I've got a few more things to gather. Why don't you take him out for a quick stroll before we leave?"

"Sure thing," she said as she

reached down and attached the leash to Bowzer's collar.

Divina joined them, flicking her tail along Bowzer's flank.

"I'll have Bowzer back in a jiffy," she said to the curious cat.

Steeling herself, Becca opened the cabin door. She gasped as freezing air whipped around her. Bowzer whined apprehensively, but didn't resist as Becca guided him out the door. She closed the door tight and stood still for a second to get her bearings.

Oh my, it was *cold*. The wind, which she'd heard faintly while in the cabin, was now a loud roar as it pushed through the trees. She felt like she had stepped into something wild and fierce and alive.

"Come on, Bowzer." With a determined step, she led her canine companion off the covered porch and into the snow-covered field. Her boots dropped deeper — much deeper — into whiteness than they had earlier. She wondered how much more snow would fall before the blizzard moved on. A gust of wind blew thick flurries of snow all around her.

Bowzer understood why they were outside and didn't dawdle. When he was finished with his business, he glanced longingly at the cabin and then her, letting her know in no uncertain terms that the cabin was where he wanted to be.

"Good boy," she said. The two of them dashed back to the porch. Becca stamped her boots and brushed her hair free of clinging snow, then opened the door and ushered them back into the mudroom. She reached down and unfastened the leash from Bowzer's collar.

Bowzer turned to get back to the warmth of the fireplace, but, when he realized Becca wasn't following, looked back at her and cocked his head inquisitively.

Becca pulled him closer and gave him a hug. "You're going to stay here with Divina. I'll be gone for awhile with Dr. Nick. I need you to behave yourself, okay?"

Bowzer looked at her, not really under-standing but wanting to please, then glanced up as Nick stepped into the mudroom with his medical bag and a duffel bag.

"Okay," Nick said, "let's go. You be a good boy, okay, Bowzer?"

"We'll be back soon," Becca said. She stood up, then followed Nick out the door. As she turned to grab the door handle, she saw that Divina had joined Bowzer to bid them farewell.

The last image she saw, as she shut the door tight, was Divina wrapping herself around Bowzer's front legs.

CHAPTER 21

*B*ecca took a deep breath, then followed Nick down a snow-covered path that wound around the cabin. Through the swirling snow, she saw Nick walk up to a free-standing three-car garage next to the cabin and pull up the middle garage door. As the door rose up, he stepped in and turned on a light, revealing a large black pickup truck with beefy wheels.

She followed him in. A quick glance around revealed a smaller hatchback utility vehicle next to the black truck. The rest of the garage looked like it was set up for woodworking and other kinds of projects.

Nick walked around to the opposite side of the black truck and bent down. Suddenly, an engine roared to life, filling the garage with noise and vibrations.

She stepped around the truck to see what he was doing and gasped.

He was bent over — a snowmobile!

"We're taking *that*?" she yelled over the sound of the engine. The machine was black and white and looked very powerful, with skis jutting out in front and thick black chains and treads at the base. There was seating for a driver and a passenger, she saw, with a small backrest for the passenger.

A flare of panic rose within her. He'd tried to warn her when he told her that the passenger seat wasn't what she was expecting. She'd never ridden a snowmobile before. How was she going to manage herself on something like *that*?

Satisfied by the sounds he was hearing, he stood, then yanked up the garage door next to the snowmobile. When he turned, his gaze landed on her face. "You don't have to do this," he yelled over the engine's roar. "The cabin's real comfy compared to what's out there."

The temptation to turn and dash back into the cozy cabin was almost impossible to resist. What if she fell off this thing? What if they crashed? She had no idea how snowmobiles worked or how they felt or what was involved or —

Stop it, she told herself. *Calm thyself down, girl.*

She took a deep breath, held it for a long second, then exhaled, waiting for her heart rate to dial back to some semblance of normal. Nick was looking at her, waiting for her to respond. His face held no judgment. She knew he'd be fine, even relieved, if she turned tail and dashed back into the cabin. Part of him, she sensed, wanted her to do just that. He had a lot on his mind right now; knowing she was safe and sound in the cabin meant one less thing for him to worry about.

But in that moment, she realized something else. He'd told her she *could* come, despite the fact that he easily could have told her she couldn't. He easily could have told her the storm made conditions too dangerous for him to bring a passenger, and she would have accepted that statement as the truth. But he hadn't said that, which meant that he was okay with bringing a passenger. No doubt he was an experienced driver, and knew how to get through the storm safely to Angus's farm.

His agreeing to bring her also meant that at least part of him *wanted* her to come. Of course, he was still concerned about how she'd respond to riding on a snowmobile — a concern she shared as well! But he was on board with the idea of her jumping on board this machine and riding with him out into a winter storm.

So the question was: How ready was *she* for another adventure?

She took another deep breath, then exhaled again, the sharp cold air filling her lungs.

And heard herself say, in a voice steadier than she had any right to expect, "Let's do this."

No question about it: craziest Christmas ever!

He gave her a grin, then walked behind the snowmobile and grabbed what looked like a small pod on skis.

"What's that?" she said.

"It's a sled for the gear," he said as he hitched the ski-pod to the back of the snowmobile. "You never know what you might need on a house call. Better safe than sorry." He opened the hatch of the pod — revealing a seat inside — and loaded in his vet bag and the duffel bag. He grabbed another duffel bag from under a work bench and tossed it in as well, then shut the pod door.

"Engine's warmed up," he yelled. "Ready?"

No, she almost admitted. But instead she said, with as much confidence as she could muster, "Ready!"

He hopped onto the snowmobile and gently throttled it out of the garage and onto the snow. She followed him outside and watched while he stepped back to the garage, shut off the light switch inside, and pulled shut the two garage doors.

His actions, she realized, were as natural and fluid and instinctive to him as categorizing and shelving books was to her. The two of them had roles to play in this small town. His role just happened to require driving snowmobiles through raging storms to save pregnant animals.

A snowflake landed on her lips and clung there for a few seconds before melting. Nick reached into the ski-pod and pulled out a helmet. He walked up to her. "Ever been on a snowmobile before?"

"Never," she said.

"Let me help you put this on." Gently, he slid the helmet over her head. It fit snugly but comfortably, with a big visor that offered protection from the wind and snow, along with a type of breathing apparatus that, she guessed, prevented the visor from getting fogged up by her breath.

"How's that feel?"

Standing so close to him, his solid presence rising before her, his hands adjusting the helmet to make sure it fastened securely around her head, she felt something she hadn't felt in quite some time: taken care of.

"It feels good," she said.

"The ride's about twenty minutes. It's mostly smooth going, but there's one stretch with twists and ups and downs. You need to hold tight to me the whole time, got it?"

"Got it."

"You need anything, just yell, okay?"

"Got it."

"Okay, let's go." He grabbed another helmet from the ski-pod and put it on, gave the ski-pod's hitch a final check to make sure it was properly attached to the snowmobile, then hopped onto the driver's seat and turned toward her, waiting.

Here goes nothing, she thought. With her heart thumping in her chest, she stepped onto the snowmobile and sat down behind Nick. She looked down to the side of the snowmobile and found a ledge for her to place her boots. The backrest pressed into her back, reassuring her with its presence. The machine beneath her throbbed impatiently, vibrations running through her.

She reached around Nick and, with gloved hands, gripped his waist tightly.

"Ready?" he yelled over his shoulder.

"Ready!" she yelled back.

And then, with a jolt and a roar — they were off!

CHAPTER 22

Becca gripped Nick's waist like her life depended on it as the machine dashed through the snow, its engine pulsing beneath her and its roar — even muffled by the helmet — nearly overwhelming her. She felt every movement, every turn, every easing and revving of the throttle. The wind and snow swirled around them, a constant reminder of the nor'easter's strength.

Her heart, fueled by adrenaline and fear, had moved into her throat and was pounding away like nobody's business. She leaned into Nick, her gloved hands holding tight to his winter coat.

Gradually, as the snowmobile made its way over the fresh snow, her heart began to settle back into its usual spot in her chest and she started to breathe in a somewhat more normal manner.

Through the darkness and swirling snow, she began to notice the scenery as they steadily chugged by.

And they were *chugging* and not racing, she realized. Perhaps because of the sled they were towing, perhaps because of her, perhaps because of the storm or the darkness or all of the above, Nick was keeping a steady, cautious pace, the engine humming along without much in the way of throbs or roars.

They were on a snow-covered road, she realized. It was probably the mountain road that led to Nick's cabin, now covered in pristine white snow, with more falling steadily. With this much fresh powder, the road was most likely impassable to all but vehicles like the one they were on now.

The powerful headlight from the snowmobile sliced through the storm, illuminating the stretch of road ahead. Somewhat to her surprise, she began to relax, reassured by Nick's careful handling. The snowmobile gripped the turns on the road easily and smoothly. The trees on either side of the road were heavy with snow. The helmet and Nick's solid presence in front of her helped protect her from most of the storm's cold wind.

From what she could tell, they seemed to be the only people out and about. She recalled what

Bert Winters had said about the snowplow not working. Until it was fixed, the only way for people to get around in weather like this was by snowmobile. Or, if they were in good shape and didn't mind a workout, by skiing or snowshoes.

Gradually, the snow-covered road began to level out. They were leaving the mountain and heading onto the flatter road of the valley outside of town. The snowmobile managed the road easily, gripping the snow and pushing them forward effortlessly.

After a few more minutes of driving, Nick slowed and came to a stop on a flat stretch of road.

"How you doing?" he yelled over his shoulder.

"Good!" she yelled back.

"We're close to the farm now. The last mile gets twisty — the road runs along a creek — so hold tight."

"Got it."

Nick gripped the throttle and — whoosh! — they were off again. Carefully, the snowmobile turned onto a side road. Through the darkness, she made out a fence running alongside them, the tips of its wooden posts topped with fresh snow. For the first time since hopping on board, she felt a smile coming to her lips. She was on quite the adventure — and so far she was doing fine.

The snowmobile descended into a steep drop, causing Becca to tighten her grip. Deftly, Nick steered the snowmobile and revved the throttle as they turned into a twist. He was right about the road — it had curves! The smile on her face faltered but didn't go away, even as more curves and dips approached. Nick took each one with aplomb, increasing Becca's confidence with every turn.

She realized she wasn't feeling fear anymore. No, what she felt instead was — exhilaration!

She laughed out loud, and Nick heard.

"You okay?" he yelled.

"I'm great!"

Up ahead, she caught sight of lights, barely visible through the swirling snow. Steadily, Nick throttled up a snow-covered driveway to a group of buildings. One of the buildings was a barn, another a farmhouse with Christmas lights twinkling through the windows. He guided them toward the barn, brought the snowmobile to a stop, and turned off the engine.

With the engine's throb gone, the sounds of the storm came roaring back. Wind whistled through the nearby trees. The barn groaned from a blast of arctic air.

Nick turned back toward her. "Need help?"

"I'm okay." Shakily, she got off the snowmobile, her boots sinking deep into the fresh snow.

She took hold of her helmet and pulled it off, gasping as frigid air hit her cheeks.

Nick hopped off the snowmobile, opened the ski-pod, and pulled out his duffel bags and medical bag. He yanked off his helmet and tossed it inside the pod, then took hers and tossed it in as well.

Becca turned as a porch light went on at the farmhouse. A side door opened and a woman, dressed in a heavy winter coat, work pants and boots, stepped out and made her way toward them.

"Howdy, Doc!" the woman said, and gestured toward the barn. "Angus is inside with Daisy."

"How's she doing?" Nick said.

"Same, no change," the woman said, and picked up one of the duffel bags. "Let's get you inside."

The woman pulled open the barn door as Nick picked up his medical bag and the second duffel bag. Quickly, they followed the woman inside the barn.

"Center stall on the left," the woman said to Nick as she shut the barn door behind them. "You go on now. This nice young lady and I can handle the introductions ourselves."

With a glance at Becca and a small grin, Nick did as he was told and headed toward the stall.

After watching him walk away, the woman

turned toward Becca. The woman was in her early sixties, with graying brown hair cut short around a square, inquisitive face. Her sharp grey eyes took in Becca with a single swift glance, and her lips twitched — perhaps with a smile, Becca couldn't tell. She stuck out her gloved hand.

"Marianne Ferguson," the woman said. "Pleased to make your acquaintance."

"Becca Jameson," Becca said, taking the woman's hand in hers.

"Ah," Marianne said, comprehension dawning. "The new librarian."

Becca nodded. "I arrived in town three days ago."

"Hettie Mae is one of my dearest friends. She's thrilled you're here to take over."

"I hope it's okay that I came here with Nick."

"Of course it is," Marianne said firmly. "A friend of Dr. Nick's is a friend of ours."

"I'm here to help, in whatever way I can."

"Good. There's plenty to do. Let's see what they need."

Marianne led the way into the center of the barn. Becca glanced around, taking in the barn's worn but well-cared-for interior. Stalls ran along one side of the barn, with bales of hay and farm equipment lining the other. Looking up, she saw big wooden beams crisscrossing the open space. Lights placed along the stalls cast a warm light over bales of hay. The smell, she realized as she breathed in, was a mix of cut hay and animals.

When they reached the stall in the center of the barn, she saw Nick and another man bent over a llama lying on the ground. Her heart lurched as she gazed upon the distressed animal. So this was Daisy! The lady llama had a thick coat of brown-and-white hair that even now looked irresistibly soft. The pregnant animal was moaning in discomfort, her eyes opening and closing, her head moving back and forth against the hay.

Becca's mouth opened slightly in surprise when she saw a leg protruding from Daisy back-side. So that was the baby, the — what did Nick call it? — the *cria*.

Next to her, Marianne said, "You ever witness a llama birth, Becca?"

"Never," Becca replied with a slow shake of her head.

Nick, bent over Daisy, was listening intently to the llama's heartbeat with a stethoscope. He moved the stethoscope from Daisy's chest to her belly and listened some more.

"Both heartbeats are elevated but steady," he said to the man kneeling next to him, who Becca expected was Marianne's husband Angus.

Marianne said, "What do you boys need from

us?" Angus looked up at his wife's use of the word "us" and his attention shifted to Becca.

"Angus," Marianne said, "this is Becca. She came with Doc. Becca, my husband Angus."

"Pleased to meet you," Becca said.

Angus gave her a brief nod, then turned back toward Daisy and her cria, his brow furrowed with worry, his bald pate gleaming in the light.

Nick stood up. "The cria's right front leg is in the wrong position. We need to get it repositioned."

"Is Daisy going to get through this, Doc?" Angus asked, anxiety in his voice.

"She should be fine," Nick said. "I brought most of what I need." He turned to Marianne and Becca. "But we'll also need towels. And we all need to wash our hands thoroughly."

"The barn has a sink along the wall," Marianne said. "Becca and I will get the towels."

"We'll need a blow dryer as well, in case the cria's body temperature is too low. Also a big plastic bag."

"Got it."

"Does the sink out here run hot water?"

"No, just cold."

"Let's get hot water into the sink in the house. If the cria's body temp is too low when she's born, we'll need to raise it."

"We'll get that ready."

Nick turned his attention to his gear, his expression serious, his focus singleminded. Becca had noticed that level of concentration from him before — how the rest of the world seemed to vanish when he zeroed in on something important.

Becca realized that Marianne was already walking toward the farmhouse, so she hurried to catch up. Marianne pulled open the barn door again, and Becca stepped out into the cold night. Marianne followed and shut the door behind her.

"Have you ever had a llama with a difficult birth before?" Becca asked Marianne as they tramped through fresh snow toward the farmhouse.

"Just once," Marianne said. "Most llama births are easy. The mama stands there and the baby cria basically just slides out." She let out a short laugh. "A lot easier than the three labors I went through, I can tell you that."

"So, you have three kids?"

"All grown up now, two with young families of their own, the youngest in college."

Becca gestured back to the barn. "What about the time you had a llama birth that didn't go easy?"

Marianne shrugged. "Luckily, we had Dr. Nick. He was here and saved two lives." She reached the door on the side of the farmhouse and pulled it open, ushering Becca into a warm and homey kitchen, brightly lit and decorated country-style. On the white fridge, held up with magnets, was a blue ribbon for "Best in Show." Next to the ribbon was a photo of Angus and Marianne standing next to a very happy-looking brown-and-white llama.

Marianne saw what Becca was looking at and smiled. "That's Daisy."

Becca's eyes widened. "She looks quite cheerful."

"Especially compared with how she's feeling right now," Marianne said as she vigorously soaped up her hands in the sink. "Every summer, Heartsprings Valley has an animal fair. Daisy won for the camelid category. Of course," she added wryly, "it helped her chances that she was the only entrant in her category."

"Not many llamas in Heartsprings Valley?"

"Just our herd." Marianne grabbed a fresh hand towel from a kitchen drawer and dried her hands. "After tonight, fingers crossed, we'll be up to nine animals."

Becca slipped off her gloves. "I'll wash up next, if that's okay."

"Soap's there, next to the sink." Marianne picked up an empty basket from a spot next to fridge and placed it on the counter. "When you're done, put the soap in the basket and grab the paper towels and also the hand towels in the drawer to the right of the sink. Also, if you could rinse out the sink and start filling it with hot water, that would be great."

"Will do."

Marianne bustled out of the kitchen and Becca got busy washing her hands in the big white farmhouse sink. The warm water from the faucet ran over her soapy fingers. Her wedding ring caught the light and gleamed.

She picked up a sponge next to the counter, dribbled liquid soap over it, and set about giving the sink a good scrub. When she was satisfied that it was clean, she rinsed the sink by splashing running water over the walls. Once that was done, she pushed the stopper into the drain and watched the hot water begin to fill the sink.

Marianne returned with an armful of towels and a blow dryer. "There's an extension cord in the lower drawer to your left."

Becca finished drying her hands, then reached down and pulled open the drawer and found the cord and added it to the basket.

"I see you're married?" Marianne said, gesturing to Becca's wedding ring.

"I was. My husband died three years ago." The words came out less painfully than she expected, perhaps because of Marianne's straightforward manner.

"I'm sorry to hear that," Marianne said. For a moment, the older woman came to a stop and gave Becca her full attention. "I can only imagine how painful the past three years must have been for you."

"Thank you."

"It must be difficult moving on."

"Yes, very difficult."

Marianne gave her shoulder a sympathetic squeeze. "You'll know when you're ready."

Becca blinked, then said, "The voice of experience?"

"If living on a farm has taught me anything, it's that anything can and will happen. And that no matter what does happen, life keeps marching on."

Becca swallowed an upsurge of unexpected emotion. "There was a time I didn't believe that. But now, I think you might be right."

Marianne nodded. "Good to hear. I try to stay focused on the here and now, with an eye on what's next. Keeps me sane." She gestured to the ring. "Probably best to take that off for now. Don't want it to get caught on anything."

"Of course," Becca said, slipping the ring off her finger. She watched Marianne placed it on the counter, next to the fridge.

"Okay to keep it here for safekeeping?" Marianne said.

"Sure."

Marianne glanced at the basket. "We got everything?"

"Yep."

Marianne looked at the sink, now three-quarters full of hot water, and turned the faucet off. "We'll adjust the temperature as needed, if and when it's time."

"Okay."

"You got the basket?"

"Yep."

Marianne picked up the towels and held open the kitchen door. "After you."

CHAPTER 23

a blast of cold air greeted them as they stepped outside the farmhouse and made their way back to the barn. Becca stepped carefully through the snow, conscious as ever about slipping and falling.

Marianne pulled the barn door open, then shut it once Becca was in. Together, they made their way to the stall, where Nick was already hard at work, doing his best to very carefully get the cria's leg into the right position. Daisy groaned with pain, her cries weak. She was clearly exhausted by her ordeal, her head rolling forward and back, her moans tearing into Becca's heart.

After what seemed like forever but what Becca realized later was only a few minutes, Nick pulled back and said, "Okay, we're good."

Daisy groaned again, her body straining to move the baby along, and this time her hard work was rewarded. Two front legs appeared, followed seconds later by the cria's snout.

"Oh, thank goodness!" Marianne said. Angus looked up with a big grin on his face.

"Got everything ready?" Nick asked Marianne.

"We're ready."

They didn't have long to wait after that. The baby llama emerged quickly, the head followed by shoulders and torso and finally the legs — a wet and gloppy mess, but a joyous one at that!

"Make sure the cria's nose and mouth are unobstructed," Nick said. Marianne reached down with a towel and carefully cleared out the baby's nose. They all breathed a sigh of relief when the baby gasped and wheezed its very first breath.

Everything sped up after that. Marianne and Angus grabbed towels to dry off the cria, Nick checked the baby's condition and announced it was a girl. Becca, meanwhile, grabbed the extension cord, found an outlet, and ran the cord to the stall and plugged in the blow dryer.

"Her temperature is too low," Nick said. "Where's the blow dryer?"

"Right here," Becca said, handing it to him.

He gave her an appreciative look. "Thinking

ahead. I like that." He turned on the blow dryer and aimed it over the baby llama's tiny body. "Here," he said, indicating for Becca to take over. "Run the air over her. Not too close, not too far." She took the dryer from him and made a couple of sweeps. "That's good."

Nick turned his attention back to Daisy.

"How's our mama llama doing, Doc?" Angus said.

"She's exhausted," Nick said, his stethoscope on, listening intently to Daisy's heartbeat. "But so far, so good. We'll know more when she passes the afterbirth."

"How long for that?"

"Anytime in the next few hours. In the meantime, we'll keep a close eye on her."

Next to Daisy, the new baby cria was breathing well. Nick turned his attention back to her and took her temperature again. He shook his head. "Still too low."

"Should we take her inside?" Marianne asked.

"Is the sink in the farmhouse ready? Filled with warm water?"

Marianne nodded.

"Good. Let's get the cria nice and dry, then into the plastic bag, and then into the warm water."

He rummaged through his duffel bag and

found a baby bottle. "Angus and I will get the colostrum and bring it in."

Marianne and Angus finished drying the baby, then slid a black plastic garbage bag over her, covering her so that only her head stuck out. Lovingly, they wrapped her bag-clad tiny body in a fresh towel.

Angus picked up the baby, then turned to Becca. "Here you go, young lady."

Becca gulped, but immediately set down the blow dryer, knelt, and took the swaddled baby llama in her arms. The baby looked up at her with the softest eyes that Becca had ever seen. Oh my, her heart was going to melt! Truly, this was turning into the most eventful Christmas ever. Just being here was such an unexpected gift. She knelt in the hay-filled stall in a trance, the baby llama resting her head on her shoulder, every tiny breath like music to her ears. She could just sit here in this moment forever, just her and the baby and —

She heard a cough then, and looked up to see Nick, Marianne and Angus staring at her patiently, waiting for her to snap out of her reverie, regarding her with a mixture of under-standing and amusement.

"Oh my," she said. "Yes, of course. Let's get inside!" She stood up and followed Marianne out of the barn, stepping carefully through the snow with the precious cargo in her arms. Marianne opened the kitchen door and Becca slipped inside and made her way to the big farmhouse sink. Marianne reached in and hand-tested the water temperature. "Just right," she said, then gestured to her. "We might get wet. Let's get you out of that coat."

Carefully, Becca passed the baby to Marianne, then shrugged off her coat and placed it on the kitchen table.

"Now," Marianne said, "we need to get this little girl into the warm water."

"I can do it, if you'd like."

"You sure? You'll get wet."

"That's fine — no worries."

"Okay, roll up your sleeves and let's get started."

Becca rolled up the sleeves of her turtleneck sweater and stepped in to take the baby llama back into her arms. The baby mewled softly, her beautiful eyes staring up at her, as Becca lowered her in. The baby blinked rapidly and moaned again as she reacted to the warmth, then sighed — with relief, it seemed — as the warm water began to have its intended effect.

"Good job," Marianne said to Becca. "The cria seems to like you, which is good." Together, they waited for the cria to slowly gain strength as the warm water helped her body temperature rise to normal.

"I heard Nick use a word I'm not familiar with," Becca said. "What's colostrum?"

"It's the first milk from a new mama," Marianne said. "It's rich in the nutrients and antibodies that the cria needs to develop her immune system."

"So Nick and Angus are ... milking Daisy now to get colostrum?"

"That's right. Once the cria's body temperature is normal, she should be able to drink the colostrum and absorb the nutrients."

"And once she has some colostrum in her, she'll have the energy to nurse from Daisy herself?"

"That's the plan."

"Thank you for letting me help you," Becca said. "I've learned so much. I've never done anything like this — ever. Farming life is way more exciting than I ever would have expected."

Marianne chuckled. "Sometimes I'd prefer a bit less excitement. I'm always relieved and grateful when a crisis results in a blessing."

The cria chose that moment to bleat softly, as if agreeing.

Becca looked down at the adorable creature nestled against her arm. "A true Christmas gift — that's what you are."

"You might even call her a Christmas miracle," Marianne said. "If Doc hadn't made it out here, we could have lost her and her mama."

"Well, that didn't happen," Becca said, glued to the baby in her arms. "Do you have a name for her?"

"I don't name my babies until I see them with my own eyes," Marianne said. She looked silently at the baby for a long moment. A smile appeared on her face. "All right, her name just came to me."

Becca said, "I'm all ears."

"We're going to name her Rebecca."

Becca's eyebrows shot up. "Rebecca?"

"In honor of a very nice young lady who helped bring new life into the world tonight."

Tears threatened. "Rebecca was my great-grandmother's name. I'm named after her."

"You don't mind?"

"I'm honored," Becca said, getting a little choked up. "This little lady here in my arms is the sweetest thing ever."

CHAPTER 24

They heard the kitchen door open and Nicked stepped in, a gust of winter air pushing in behind him. He took a bottle of mother's milk from inside his coat and handed it to Marianne, then stepped up to the sink next to Becca and checked the baby llama's temperature. "Good," he said. "She's warming up nicely."

He took the bottle from Marianne. "Let's see if this little gal is ready to drink." He rubbed a bit of the colostrum on the nipple of the bottle, then brought the bottle to the baby's mouth. The baby, reacting instinctively to the smell and taste, took the nipple into her mouth and started sucking down the colostrum.

Becca gasped. "She's drinking it."

"She sure is," Nick said.

"How's Daisy?" Marianne asked.

"Back on her feet," Nick said.

"No afterbirth?"

"Not yet. Fingers crossed, sometime soon."

Marianne looked out the window. "I just realized your snowmobile is out in the snow. I'll run it into the garage."

"I can do that," Nick said.

"No, let me," she said. "You stay here with Becca and Rebecca."

He nodded, reached into his pocket and handed her the keys. Then he realized what Marianne had said. "Rebecca?"

Marianne gave him a smile. "Nice name, isn't it?" Without another word, she headed out to take care of the snowmobile.

In Becca's arms, the baby llama was suckling ferociously on the bottle.

Nick turned toward her, a grin on his face. "Rebecca?"

"Could have knocked me over with a feather," Becca said. "She named her out of the blue."

From outside, they heard the roar of the snowmobile's engine.

"What's next for Daisy and Rebecca?" Becca asked.

Nick's expression became serious. "Daisy needs to pass her afterbirth. After that happens, she needs to let Rebecca start nursing."

"Is any of that difficult?"

"Not usually. Natural instinct kicks in most of the time. But these two have just been through a rough birth. We'll have to keep a close eye."

The baby shifted in her arms. The colostrum in the bottle was almost gone.

"You've done really well tonight," he said. "You didn't hesitate to jump right in."

"I'm glad I was able to help."

She gazed up into his deep brown eyes. There was an intensity there. She saw appreciation and respect and fondness, along with — her heart leaped —

At that second the kitchen door whipped open and Marianne dashed back in. A cold gust of air filled the room. "Got the snowmobile into the garage," she said as she shut the door tight. "Boy, this storm's a doozy."

"Thanks," Nick said, shifting back into veterinarian mode. "Rebecca's taking the colostrum well."

"Good," Marianne said.

"When she's done with the bottle, we'll bring her back to the barn."

"And then?"

"We wait."

"The bottle's almost empty," Becca said.

"Excellent," Nick said. He watched the baby finish off the last drops, then put the bottle back into his coat pocket. "I can carry her out there, if you want."

"No, I'll take her," Becca said.

"Hold your horses, young lady," Marianne said. "Your arm is soaked. Before you go outside, let's get you into something warm and dry."

Becca gave Nick a smile as Marianne hustled out of the kitchen. "Marianne's really great."

"She sure is," Nick said. He looked at her like he wanted to say something — like he wanted to return to the moment they'd had before Marianne burst in — but he heard Marianne's footsteps returning and held off.

Marianne carried in a towel, long-sleeved undershirt, and red sweater. "Doc and I can get Rebecca out of the water while you dry off. You can step into the other room to change into these dry clothes."

Becca paused, instinctively rebelling about letting go of the baby llama.

"We've got her," Nick said gently. "Scoot."

Becca sighed. "Okay." Slowly, she removed her arm from the sink and let Nick and Marianne move in to support baby Rebecca. Arm dripping, she grabbed the towel and dried herself off, then picked up the undershirt and sweater and headed into the next room, which turned out to be the dining room.

Quickly, she changed into the long undershirt,

then shrugged into the red sweater. From where she stood next to the dining table, she could hear Marianne and Nick talking, though she couldn't make out the words.

She stepped back into the kitchen, picked up her heavy winter coat, and slipped into it. "Ready to go," she said.

Marianne nodded and, with Nick's help, took the baby llama out of the warm sink. Quickly, they dried the plastic bag covering the baby's body and wrapped her in a fresh towel.

"Here we go," Marianne said as she placed the baby in Becca's arms.

"Hey, girl," Becca cooed to her little namesake.

"You two are so adorable together. Don't you agree, Doc?"

"Completely adorable," Nick said immediately. When Becca's gaze met his, he blushed and shifted back into vet mode. "Let's get going."

Together, they returned to the barn. When Becca reached the stall, she saw that Daisy was back on her feet, with Angus next to her, whispering softly in her ear. "Look who's back," he said to her. "Your brand-new baby girl."

Nick said, "Okay, I'll take her from here." Becca handed him the baby. He stepped into the stall, set the baby llama on the hay, carefully removed her from the plastic bag, then stood back.

"Okay, little gal," he said, "time to stand up."

Baby Rebecca looked at Nick quizzically before turning her head toward her mother. Daisy looked at her baby with interest, then stepped forward to nuzzle her.

The baby llama bleated and her little legs moved. Guided by instinct, she twisted her legs into position and, wobbling and shaking, rose from the hay.

Or least tried to. With a bleat of surprise, the baby llama stumbled and fell back into the hay.

"Oh no!" Becca said.

"It happens," Marianne said. "She'll try again."

Becca's eyes filled again with tears as the baby llama recovered from her tumble. She bleated again, then moved her legs into position and —

Stood up!

Wobbling wildly, Baby Rebecca lurched sideways, her legs moving awkwardly beneath her as she tried to remain standing. She turned her head to look at her mother, then stumbled into Daisy's front legs.

Becca's heart jumped with concern. What if Baby Rebecca fell again?

But falling again didn't appear to be in the cards — not if this little gal had anything to say about it. Almost by the second, the baby's sense of balance seemed to improve.

Angus thumped Nick on the back. "Look at her, Doc," he said. "She's doing great."

Marianne said, "Now for her mama."

"Daisy needs to start nursing, right?" Becca asked.

"That's right," Marianne said, "but first she needs to pass her afterbirth."

"How soon before that happens?"

"Hopefully soon," Marianne said. She turned to Angus. "How about I get us some of that Christmas Eve dinner we were about to enjoy when Daisy decided to interrupt us?"

"You read my mind."

Marianne turned to Becca. "Becca, you want to help?"

"Of course!" Becca said.

"Back to the farmhouse we go."

CHAPTER 25

*I*t ended up being the most unusual Christmas Eve dinner that Becca had ever had. Back in the kitchen, she and Marianne used the microwave to reheat hearty helpings of cornbread stuffing, mashed potatoes, and green bean casserole, along with thick slices of home-made bread and honeyed ham.

"We were supposed to go to my daughter's place across town for dinner," Marianne explained, "but when the storm hit, we realized we were stuck, so I started getting dinner ready for just the two of us. Angus went out to check on Daisy, and that's when our plans for a nice quiet Christmas Eve dinner went out the window."

Becca breathed in the aroma of the homemade food. "Everything smells so delicious."

Marianne smiled, then set a basket on the

kitchen table. "Let's get everything into the basket. I'll get plates and napkins and utensils."

Becca added the containers of hot food to the basket.

"One more thing, and we're ready," Marianne said as she slipped a thermos into the basket, along with four mugs.

"What's that's?" Becca asked, curious.

"A Christmas surprise," Marianne said with a smile.

Becca grinned. "I love Christmas surprises." She picked up the basket. "I'll carry."

"You sure? It's heavy."

"I got it."

With Marianne leading the way, they made their way back to the barn. When they returned to Daisy's stall, Becca saw the mama llama and her new baby nuzzling each other.

"Any nursing yet?" Marianne asked.

"Not yet," Angus said. "No afterbirth yet."

"So we ... wait?" Becca said.

"We wait," Angus said, eyeing the basket of food. "Doc, let's wash up."

The two men went to the barn's sink and soaped up while Becca knelt next to the basket. She took out the plates and set them and utensils on top of paper towels on a bale of hay.

Nick and Angus returned, and the four of them, using bales of hay as seating, dug into the hot food, filling their plates with the delicious Christmas dinner.

"Mmmm," Nick said, his mouth full of stuffing. "This is amazing, Marianne."

"Oh, my," Becca said as delicious mashed potatoes tingled her taste buds, "this is so good!"

"I'm a lucky man to be married to this woman," Angus said as he tore into the honeyed ham.

Marianne smiled with pleasure. "I'm just happy we're all here to celebrate a joyous occasion." She picked up the thermos and opened it, then poured the drink inside into the four mugs. One by one, she handed them a mug.

Becca brought hers close to her nose and breathed in. Heated air scented with cinnamon and spice filled her lungs. Hot apple cider — so heavenly!

"A toast," Marianne said, "to Dr. Nick."

"To the doc!" Angus said.

With a modest nod, Nick accepted the toast, and together the four of them drank.

Warmth rushed through Becca as the cider did its magic. What a perfect treat to have in this hay-filled barn, after a long evening of caring for a wonderful pair of animals. The barn creaked from a gust of wind, a reminder of the storm still swirling outside.

Angus set his mug down and looked at Nick.

With a quick glance at Becca and a twinkle in his eye, he said, "Sorry we interrupted your date, Doc."

Nick blinked with surprise. "Oh," he said quickly. "We weren't on a date."

"No, not a date," Becca said, rushing to agree with him, her heart suddenly racing.

"Becca and Bowzer were caught in the snowstorm," Nick explained to Marianne and Angus.

"We were a bit lost, to be honest," Becca added right away.

"I was out chopping wood."

"And Bowzer caught his scent."

"Suddenly, Bowzer came bounding up."

"He got off the leash."

"He took me by surprise."

"But I was so grateful Nick was there," Becca said.

"I knew they needed to be out of the storm."

"And Nick offered us shelter in his cabin."

"I was happy to help out."

"And I was grateful."

"We were making hot cocoa when you radioed," Nick said.

"His grandmother's recipe. So delicious."

"Just hanging out by the fire."

"Bowzer was getting to know Nick's cat, Divina."

"So it wasn't a date," Nick said.

"Nope, not a date at all," Becca agreed.

She and Nick stopped their rushed explanations and waited for Angus and Marianne to respond. For a long second, the farming couple didn't move a muscle.

Then they both laughed!

"Not a date?" Angus said, and laughed some more.

"Oh, you two," Marianne added.

A perplexed-but-pleased look appeared on Nick's face, like he was confused about why his story was being challenged but at the same time was enjoying it.

As for herself, Becca knew her face was flaming red. Her cheeks always betrayed her when she was feeling self-conscious. And she was certainly feeling self-conscious right now!

Marianne noticed and chuckled some more, but mercifully decided to back off. "Okay, Angus and I will stop teasing. You two are new friends — that's all. Message received, loud and clear."

Becca glanced at her "new friend" and found him already looking at her. Their eyes locked for a long second before Becca tore her gaze away. "Marianne," she said briskly, "this hot apple cider is delicious. Would you mind sharing the recipe?"

Marianne gave her a knowing look but merely said, "Of course."

Angus was about to add something when a

moan from the stall diverted him. He rose to his feet and looked in. "Good news — the afterbirth's here."

Nick stood and followed his gaze. "And it's looking normal," he said after a moment. "A good sign."

Curious about what it looked like, Becca walked up the stall and saw a big red gloppy mess protruding from Daisy's backside. A bit gross, if she was being honest, but also fascinating. "What comes next?"

"Fingers crossed," Nick said, "what comes next is that Daisy allows baby Rebecca to nurse."

CHAPTER 26

*M*arianne began gathering up the plates, and Becca moved to help her.

"No, young lady," Angus said, "you stay here with Doc."

"You sure?" Becca said.

Angus nodded, so Becca returned her attention to the stall. Daisy moaned softly and took several steps forward.

"Do she need our help?" Becca asked Nick, gesturing toward the afterbirth that was still not yet fully expelled.

"No," Nick said. "It's best if she expels it on her own."

Next to her mother, baby Rebecca was gaining confidence in her newfound walking skills. With every awkward step, she seemed to be getting stronger and more surefooted.

"How about the baby llama?" Becca asked. "She doing okay?"

Nick nodded. "She's doing great. Looks like the colostrum went down well."

"So the only remaining big step is ... nursing?"

"That's right. As soon as the afterbirth is expelled, Daisy should allow Rebecca to nurse."

She heard the barn door open and shut as Marianne and Angus took what was left of the Christmas Eve dinner back to the farmhouse. For the first time since arriving at the farm, she and Nick were alone.

She felt it then — a hint of the self-consciousness that had hit her before. The feeling intensified as his focus turned toward her. "Thank you for everything you've done here tonight," he said. "You've been a huge help."

"Oh, I was happy to pitch in. I've never done anything like this before — I'm grateful I had the opportunity."

Daisy chose that moment to moan softly again. Nick gestured to the two llamas. "I'm relieved these two gals are doing as well as they are. They've had a rough day."

"If you had asked me yesterday about what I'd be doing on Christmas Eve, never in a million years would I guessed I'd be in a hay-filled barn with a mama llama and her brand-new baby."

Nick grinned. "What did you expect you'd be doing?"

"Oh, that's easy. I thought I'd be in my cottage in front of a roaring fire, decorating a gingerbread house to bring to Hettie Mae's tomorrow."

"You're going to Hettie Mae's for Christmas Day dinner?"

"She wanted to make sure I didn't spend Christmas Day alone."

"I'm glad to hear that. I wouldn't want you to spend Christmas alone either."

She was about to ask Nick about his plans for Christmas Day when she heard the barn door open. Marianne and Angus were back.

"Storm's passing," Angus said.

"How's Daisy?" Marianne said.

All of them turned toward the mama llama. At that very moment, the afterbirth fell onto the hay.

Becca's gasped, and Marianne let loose with a pleased "Hurrah!"

Nick put on a pair of gloves. "Do you have another plastic bag?"

"Sure thing," Marianne said. She turned toward the basket of supplies that she and Becca had gathered earlier that evening. Nick took a bag from and stepped into the stall and quickly gathered the afterbirth.

"Did I read somewhere that some animals eat their afterbirth?" Becca asked.

Nick nodded. "Some do, but not llamas. We'll get this out of here to make sure it doesn't attract foxes or coyotes." He tied up the bag and handed it to Angus, then turned back toward Daisy and gave her a quick examination.

Satisfied, he said, "Let's see if she's ready to nurse." He turned around and gently guided baby Rebecca to her mother's belly, then stood back.

Baby Rebecca didn't need any help after that. Instinctively, the little lady seemed to know exactly what to do. Her snout and mouth zeroed in on her mother's tender teats and —

She began nursing!

Daisy's head whipped around to look at her new baby and —

She allowed her baby to nurse!

"Oh my!" Becca gasped.

Angus laughed with relief. Marianne sighed and clasped her hands. Together, the four of them watched mom and daughter bond as the little one drank more of the life-affirming goodness of her mother's milk.

"You did it, Doc!" Marianne said.

Angus was beaming. "These two wouldn't

have made it without you. Thanks so much for coming out through this storm."

"Just doing my job," Nick said.

"Oh, what a relief," Marianne said.

Nick stepped out of the stall. "Looks like these two are going to be okay. No more need for us to stand vigil out here." He bent down to repack his duffel bags and vet kit. "Maybe you could check on them before you go to bed?"

"Sure thing," Marianne said.

While Nick finished packing, Becca stepped closer to the nursing baby. "Bye bye, little Rebecca. I'll come see you soon."

Little Rebecca was too busy drinking her mama's milk to pay attention, but Daisy noticed, extending her head toward Becca and sniffing the air inquisitively.

"Daisy's normally a very curious gal," Angus said. "I can tell by her interest in you that she's starting to feel better."

"Good," Becca said.

When Nick finished packing, the four humans left the barn and trudged through the snow to the farmhouse. Angus was right about the storm. The wind was weaker now, the snow barely falling.

As they stepped into the kitchen, Marianne said, "The two of you are welcome to stay the night. Won't take but a minute to make up the guest rooms."

Nick shook his head. "The storm's passing. I can use the snowmobile to get Becca back to her cottage."

Becca blinked. She hadn't given a second's thought to where she'd be spending the night. She realized she'd unconsciously assumed that she and Bowzer would crash on the couch in Nick's cabin. Returning home was, of course, the sensible way to conclude her Christmas Eve adventures. So why did that plan seem deflating? Why did she suddenly feel ... disappointed?

Three pairs of eyes swung her way, and she realized they were all waiting for her to respond. "Of course," she said. "If that's okay with you, Nick."

"Happy to," Nick said.

"You got everything?" Marianne asked him.

"I think so. I'll go get the snowmobile started." He turned to Becca. "See you out there in a minute?"

"Sure thing."

"I'll give you a hand," Angus said.

The two men left.

"I'm packing leftovers for both of you," Marianne said.

"You don't have to do that," Becca protested.

"Nonsense. Won't take but a minute." Quickly and efficiently, Marianne filled plastic containers with hefty helpings of Christmas leftovers and slipped them into a shopping bag. "There," she said.

"Thank you for this. And for everything else, too."

Marianne pulled Becca in for a hug. "Young lady, thank *you*. You pitched right in and we really appreciate it."

"I'm so glad I was able to help," Becca said as she returned the other woman's hug.

Marianne squeezed some more. "We're so glad you're here, Becca. Welcome to Heartsprings Valley!"

Becca laughed. "Thank you."

"I hope you're feeling happy about moving here."

"Oh, I am," Becca replied as she finally stepped back.

"You got everything?"

Becca looked around as she wrapped her scarf around her neck and zippered up her winter coat. "I think so."

Marianne turned toward the kitchen counter and picked up Becca's wedding ring. "Don't forget this important memento."

"Oh, thank you," Becca said.

Marianne slipped the ring into Becca's winter coat pocket, then gripped her by the shoulder and looked her in the eye.

"You're ready, you know," the older woman said.

Becca's heart thumped. "I'm not sure what you mean," she stammered, even though she knew exactly what Marianne was referring to.

"I think you do," Marianne said with a smile, then gave her another hug. "Now scoot. The doc is waiting for you!"

CHAPTER 27

*M*inutes later, they were off! Becca glanced over her shoulder at Angus and Marianne waving goodbye. Becca held tight to Nick's waist as he steered the snowmobile expertly through the twists and turns of the road.

The roaring winds of the nor'easter had faded away. The night was clear and quiet now, the only sound in Becca's ears the gentle throb of the snowmobile as it smoothly made its way over the fresh snow. Above them, the moon's pale light reflected off the pristine snowfall, casting everything in a soft silvery glow.

Her earlier anxieties about being on a snowmobile were long gone. Now that she knew what to expect, she felt herself really starting to enjoy herself. Nick was a skilled driver, and he was deliberately maintaining a careful pace. The unblemished beauty of Heartsprings Valley's winter wonderland greeted her no matter where she looked.

Gradually, the road rose from the valley as they headed toward Nick's mountain cabin. Almost too soon, they were there. Nick eased them onto the driveway, turned off the engine, and stepped off the snowmobile. "Sit tight," he said. "Won't take but a minute." She turned and watch him unload the ski-pod. He picked up the two duffel bags and medical kit and carried them to the garage, then set them down and pulled open the garage door with a single sure movement. He made it all look so easy, his actions smooth and effortless.

He stowed his gear into the garage, then pulled the garage door back down. "I'll get Bowzer," he said.

Becca stood up to stretch her legs, then stepped off the snowmobile to check out the empty ski-pod. Inside the pod was a seat for a passenger. The pod itself had a windshield of sorts to let the passenger see outside and enjoy the view.

She heard a joyful bark and turned around to see Bowzer bounding toward her.

"Bowzer!" she said with a laugh as the dog ran

into her arms. "How are you? Did you and Divina had good time?"

Bowzer answered with another happy bark before he started sniffing her legs and arms intently. Had he noticed the scent of baby Rebecca? Maybe someday she'd be able to introduce the two of them. How interesting it would be if, just for a day, she could experience the world like he did.

Nick returned from the cabin.

"How's everything inside?" Becca asked.

"All good. The queen and her new buddy behaved themselves."

She laughed and have Bowzer a pat. "Good boy."

He gestured to the pod. "Let's get this guy inside so we can get you two home."

"Okay, boy," she said as she took hold of his collar and led him toward the pod, "hop in."

Bowzer wasn't sure at first what she wanted, but he let himself be guided into the pod. He looked around the interior as he stepped in, then gave them a perplexed look as Nick shut the pod door.

"You ready, Bowzer?" Becca said. From inside the pod, the big guy cocked his head and stared at her quizzically.

Nick settled into driver's seat. "Ready?"

Becca hopped in behind him and grabbed his waist. "Ready!"

Nick turned on the snowmobile and, with a gentle turn of the throttle, eased them forward.

As they reached the road, she glanced back to check on Bowzer and found him looking right back at her, mouth open, tongue lolling, eyes ablaze with curiosity and excitement. He was enjoying his first snowmobile ride way more than she had!

With a smile on her face, she turned back around. Her gloved hands gripped Nick's waist as she settled in. Never in a million years would she have imagined being where she was right now. Every turn of the road, every rev of the motor, every rush of cold night air, brought her closer to truly experiencing the joy of the moment as it was happening.

The memory of holding that darling baby llama in her arms flashed before her, creating such a feeling of warmth inside that she suddenly felt invincible against the winter freeze. That little baby animal, with her big soft eyes, looking up at her with so much innocent trust and love — oh, her heart had melted right then and there. And when Marianne had named her *Rebecca* — such an unexpected Christmas gift.

She gripped Nick's waist tighter and leaned

into his strong back. He noticed right away and turned back and yelled, "Everything okay?"

"Everything's perfect!" she yelled back, not budging an inch.

"There in a few!"

Indeed, the twinkling lights of Heartsprings Valley were fast approaching. As they reached the outskirts of town, Nick slowed and, as quietly as possible, drove them down the silent streets, past houses that were mostly dark, the residents fast asleep. The fresh snowfall reflected the glow of the festive Christmas displays — prancing reindeer, jolly snowmen, huge candy canes, and colorful lights decorating houses and wrapping trees and lining walkways.

She didn't even know what time it was, but it had to be approaching midnight. Though the nor'easter had moved on, it had certainly left a hefty reminder of its power. The town would wake up to a whole lot of snow on Christmas Day!

As the snowmobile turned onto her street, she knew she wasn't ready for the ride to end. She wanted it to go on. She wanted more of what she was experiencing right now.

But all too soon, she caught a glimpse of her adorable cottage, now fully covered by fresh snow. Nick brought the snowmobile to a stop and shut off the engine.

The gentle whoosh of silence filled her ears. For a long second, neither she nor Nick moved.

A wave of self-consciousness washed over her as she realized her hands were still tightly gripping Nick's waist and she was still leaning into his back. Regretfully, she pulled away and stood up. Carefully, her legs taking a second or two to adjust, she stepped off the snowmobile, gasping with surprise as her boots sank nearly a foot into fresh snow.

"Oh my!" she said. "Look how snow much we got."

Nick followed her off the snowmobile. He removed his helmet and looked around at the quiet street, a big grin on his face.

"Lots of shoveling tomorrow," he said.

She smiled and removed her helmet as well. She liked that big wide grin of his. It transformed his handsome face, showing that he was relaxed — that he was enjoying himself.

The helmet had mussed up his shaggy brown hair. Without even thinking about what she was doing, she reached up to straighten the thick locks. As her hand brushed the hair from his forehead, he went still, his mood shifting from relaxation to alertness to — something more.

She had his full and undivided attention now. His deep brown eyes didn't waver from hers. He was so tall — so solid and strong and assured. She found it hard to breathe. *What was she doing?*

He leaned in toward her, his lips approaching hers —

Until she gasped and pulled away.

"I'm sorry," she said, taking a step back. "I didn't mean —"

"Didn't mean what?" he asked quietly.

She forced herself to look up and hold his gaze. "It's been such a long day. I know you must be worn out."

His brown eyes regarded her steadily. "I'm not tired."

"Oh," she said, then realized what he meant. "*Oh.*"

The mix of emotions that roared through her in that moment — panic mixed with surprise and eagerness — felt fresh but also familiar.

And oh-so-*confusing*.

He seemed to see every emotion that flitted across her face. "I can tell you're anxious to get inside," he said, taking a step back, patience and understanding in his tone. He looked at her with unmistakable affection.

He reached down and took her hands in his. "I'm really glad you moved to Heartsprings Valley, Becca." He squeezed her hands. "Really glad."

Her cheeks flushed red. "Likewise," she stammered. "I want to thank you for everything you've done for me today, and for Bowzer."

"Let's get you guys inside."

He stepped to the ski pod and unfastened the door to let Bowzer out. Bowzer jumped into the snow and nuzzled his head against Nick's leg, then turned to Becca.

"Good boy," she said as she leaned down to give him a pat. "Go do your business, then let's get inside."

Her canine companion seemed to understand, bounding his way through the snow toward a nearby tree.

"Both of us are so grateful," Becca said as she handed Nick her helmet.

"Glad to be of help." He tossed her helmet into the pod and shut the pod's door, then watched the dog's slow return through the deep snow. "I think I'll swing by Bert's to see if he's still up. Maybe I can give him a hand with the snowplow."

Bowzer reached them and Nick said, "You got everything?"

"Yep," she said as she patted her pockets to check for her keys and phone.

He reached into the pod and took out two containers of leftovers. "Don't forget these."

"Thank you," she said as she took them. The two of them stood rooted in place for a few long seconds, their earlier awkwardness back in full force. Then Becca turned to Bowzer. "Let's get you inside."

She stepped through the fresh snow in her small front yard to her cottage's front door, reached into her coat for her keys, pulled them out and unlocked her door.

As Bowzer shook himself free of snow and slipped inside, Becca looked back toward Nick. "Thank you again! And Merry Christmas!"

"See you soon, Becca," Nick said. "Merry Christmas." He put his helmet back on, gave her a long look, then settled onto the snowmobile and started it up. With a gentle twist of the throttle, he turned the snowmobile around and, with a final wave, slowly drove away.

CHAPTER 28

*S*he watched his figure recede into the night, her insides churning with feelings she wasn't yet ready to face. When she could no longer see him, she stamped her boots to dislodge the snow, stepped into her cottage, and shut the door behind her.

Oh my goodness. What a day. What a night. So much had happened. So much that was wonderful and exciting and scary and surprising. So many challenges, and not just of the physical sort. Riding through a blizzard on a snowmobile was a piece of cake compared with the emotional upheaval that had suddenly gripped her.

She set the leftovers on the entry table, took off her gloves, unbuttoned her heavy winter coat, and slipped out of her boots. She unwrapped the scarf from around her neck and hung it over her coat. Spying her house slippers next to her comfy sofa, she made her way to them and slipped them on.

The fireplace was dark and the living room chilly, so she turned on the gas and watched the fire crackle to life. Almost immediately, the fire's welcome heat warmed her cheeks.

She wasn't prepared to tackle what was going on inside her — not yet — so she stood up and took the leftovers into the kitchen. She placed them in the fridge — they'd be delicious tomorrow, when she reheated them — and checked the gingerbread dough. She didn't usually allow the dough settle for twelve hours, but no matter.

By all rights, she should be exhausted. Instead, she felt a nervous energy, a restlessness, that told her she wasn't quite ready for sleep.

"I'll roll you out and get you in the oven," she said out loud to the dough. "And in the morning, I'll decorate."

She nodded, pleased that her plan would keep her busy and focused for a bit longer. Bowzer stepped into the kitchen, curious about who she was talking to. She gave him a smile. "Don't you worry. Mama's just rambling." He seemed to nod, then turned and headed back to the living room, where he jumped up onto the couch and settled in.

The next few minutes were taken up with

preparations that she knew by heart — rolling out the dough to the perfect thickness, cutting the dough into the shapes of walls and roof. Before she knew it, she found herself sliding the pan of dough into the oven and setting the timer.

What to do next? Certainly not *think*. The kitchen needed a bit of cleaning up — that was it. For the next few minutes, while the gingerbread baked, she handwashed her rolling pin and dirty dishes and cleaned the countertops. After she refreshed Bowzer's water bowl, she stepped into the living room and pulled her phone from her winter coat and plugged it into the socket to charge it up.

The *ping* of the oven's timer told her the gingerbread was ready. She leaned down in front of the oven and peered in. Yes, they were perfect. She grabbed an oven mitt, opened the oven, and pulled out the tray. Immediately, the kitchen was filled with the delicious aroma of hot gingerbread. With a smile on her face, she set the tray on top of oven to let it cool, then turned off the oven.

She stepped back into the living room to check on the fire, which was quickly turning the room toasty warm. Bowzer looked up from his spot on the sofa, wagging his tail, encouraging her to join him.

With a start, she realized her ring was missing

from the third finger of her left hand. She went to her winter coat and reached inside the pocket. Her fingers closed over the familiar band. As she pulled it out and held it, poised over her ring finger, something Marianne said came back to her. What was it she had said, exactly?

Then she remembered: When Marianne had slipped the ring into Becca's coat pocket, she hadn't referred to the ring as a ring. Instead, she'd called it a "memento." A reminder of times past.

Becca inhaled sharply, the emotional tumult she'd been trying to suppress rising powerfully within her. Was Marianne right? Was her wedding ring — her symbol of commitment to her departed husband — truly a part of her *past*?

Her heart cracked open as the question pushed through her. She felt faint, her face flushing with heat, her heart rate ratcheting up. Her marriage — was it truly part of her past? Was it — and there was no way for her to avoid this painful truth — *over*?

Her heard split open, pulled wide apart and exposed as never before, as she realized that Marianne was *right*.

A gasp escaped her throat. Tears filled her eyes.

It was time to accept, truly and finally and utterly, that her beloved husband, the first man she'd ever loved, was *gone*. She would always honor him and treasure him. She would always miss him. Every day, she would remember him. If he was looking over her now — and sometimes she sensed he was — she knew he would want her to value the life she'd been blessed with. Life wasn't just about looking back. It was also about looking forward to each day and experiencing life's simple joys — like breathing in fresh winter air, making gingerbread houses, and adopting a wonderful dog. It was about making new friends, helping her neighbors, honoring her family, and so much more. Life, her departed husband would tell her, was meant to be *lived*.

A raw sob tore through her, followed by another and another. With the ring gripped tight in her fist, she flung herself onto her sofa and cried in a way she hadn't cried in months and maybe years. The wells of grief came from deep within, so full and powerful that they pained her, her gasps for breath the only respite from the waves of emotion surging through her.

She had no idea how long she lay there sobbing, curled up in a ball, the hard edge of the wedding ring's diamond pressing into her palm, as three years of loss rolled through her. But eventually, the raging storm passed. Her breathing became less ragged.

She became aware of Bowzer next to her, gazing at her anxiously, his snout quivering with concern. Such an adorable dog. She was so lucky to have him in her life.

She reached out and pulled him in for a hug. "Hey, boy."

He gave her wrist a lick, his big friendly gaze filled with concern.

"Mama's gonna be fine. Promise."

With a deep sigh, she let him go, sat herself up, grabbed a tissue from the side table, and blew her nose. Three tissues later, still trembling but feeling somewhat more under control, she planted her feet on the floor and stood up, her canine companion closely watching her every move.

With the ring in her fist still digging into her palm, she made her way to her bedroom, to her sturdy oak dresser. The dresser had been hers since she was a little girl, ever since her grandmother had passed it on to her. Maybe someday, if she was blessed with the opportunity, she would pass the dresser to her own granddaughter.

She pulled open the top-left drawer, the sound of worn wood sliding in the groove a familiar and reassuring reminder of times past, and removed a black-velvet ring box. Biting her lip, she opened the box, which was empty inside.

Tears flowing freely, she carefully placed her wedding ring inside and pressed the lid down, gasping as the box snapped shut. She set the box in the drawer, pausing as the weight of the moment sank in.

Then she knew: She was ready. With a deep breath to give her strength, she pushed the drawer closed.

CHAPTER 29

*B*ecca groaned as a loud buzz filled her ears. Consciousness returned, along with a realization of where she was — in bed, snuggled under her thick comforter, rudely pulled from a deep sleep by her darned alarm clock. She stretched underneath the comforter, wishing she could stay buried beneath her toasty-warm blankets and keep the world at bay for just a little while longer.

Her hand shot out and found her alarm clock and hit the snooze button. She sighed with relief as the sound vanished.

Just a few more minutes of lovely sleep....

Far too abruptly, those minutes ended when the rude alarm clock interrupted her slumber yet again.

"Argh," she muttered. She popped her head

from beneath her blankets to test whether her eyelids were capable of opening, and squinted warily at the bright morning sun flooding through the windows.

Then she remembered why she'd set her alarm: It was Christmas Day! And she had so much to do!

The jolt of memory was enough to get her moving. With a groan, she sat upright. Her comforter tumbled from her. Bowzer, alerted by the sound of her moving around on the bed, trotted into the bedroom and gave her a plaintive look.

"Merry Christmas, Bowzer," she said, her voice a thick after a night of slumber.

He approached the bed and rested his head on the bed next to her, inviting her to pet him. Which of course she did, because how could she resist such cuteness?

"Okay," she said as she rubbed sleep from her eyes. "The day begins. Give mama a few minutes, then we'll get you outside for a walk."

She rolled her shoulders to loosen up and realized that yesterday's exertions had made an impact — her muscles were so sore! Probably it was because of how tightly she'd held onto Nick on the snowmobile, especially at the beginning of the ride, when everything was so new and uncertain.

She was still bone-tired — the thought of a few more hours sleep was almost irresistible — but she also realized she was feeling a bit more energetic than she had any right to expect. After the day and night she'd just had, she should be exhausted, both physically and emotionally. Perhaps the energy was there because she'd slept well, deeply and without the tossing and turning that sometimes plagued her.

Minutes later, still clad in pajamas but warmly bundled up in her heavy winter coat and scarf and gloves and boots, she and Bowzer were outside, trudging through the thick blanket of snow that the blizzard had left behind.

To her surprise, she saw that her street was already plowed. She'd been sleeping so deeply, she hadn't even heard the snowplow pass. Clearly, Bert Winters had figured out how to fix it. Maybe with Nick's help?

Several of her neighbors had already cleared their sidewalks, but most of them, like her, had some shoveling to do. Yet another task to add to her to-do list.

Bowzer's eager nose was sniffing up a storm, pausing to check every tree and bush and fence they passed. No doubt he'd be thrilled to go on another adventure. But that wasn't in the cards today, not with all the tasks she had lined up. "Okay, Bowzer, time to head back home," she said. Her canine pal looked longingly at all the trees and bushes and fences he had yet to sniff, but he didn't object when she turned them around and led them back to the cottage.

Once inside, after getting her canine pal fed and watered, she turned her attention to today's big to-do: building and decorating the gingerbread house she'd bring to Hettie Mae's for Christmas dinner. She wasn't going to have as much time as she normally allowed for decorating, so she'd have to be strategic about her choices.

First up: the crucial step of getting the walls and roof glued together with icing. She'd done this dozens of times over the years, so she knew exactly what needed to be done. For this important step, there would be no muss, no fuss, no thinking, no worrying — just a whole lot of *doing*.

She selected the necessary cooking implements and ingredients and got to work on the icing, feeling a hum of satisfaction as she whipped the ingredients together to achieve the proper consistency. In the bright light of day, with last night's storm a part of the past, she was now able to look back on her eventful day with Nick in a more measured manner. She'd read too much into everything that had happened between them yesterday. She'd put way too much pressure on herself and also him. Amidst the drama of the snowstorm, she'd turned the simple act of making hot cocoa into an important and meaningful event. In the clear light of day, she saw now that making hot cocoa was about *making hot cocoa*.

And yet.... Hadn't she felt something special? And hadn't he felt the same? She stopped stirring and gave herself an internal scolding. *No, Becca,* she admonished herself. *Stop being so susceptible to wishful thinking.* She might be ready to move forward with her life — and her gut told her she was, finally and fully — but clearly Nick wasn't. He'd quit romance just like he'd quit Christmas. His days were about immersing himself in his work and helping his neighbors. He'd been so good with Daisy and Rebecca, and so helpful to her and Bowzer, and most likely he'd also helped Bert with the snowplow. He was far too busy helping people to have time for romance.

When she saw him next, she would treat him as a new friend. Yes, that sounded right. A very sensible approach — mature and reasonable and appropriate. Sure, she allowed, maybe that approach was a bit disappointing. But she was a big girl. She was going to be just fine.

Still....

No, she told herself, very firmly. *Clear head, stout heart.*

The icing was the perfect consistency to hold

the weight of the walls and roof of the gingerbread house. When it dried, it would be like
sugared cement. With a skill borne of frequent
practice, she applied icing to the edges of two
walls and began the building process.

For the next few moments, her attention
focused fully on the task at hand, she forgot all
about her newfound resolve to maintain friendly
relations with handsome veterinarians.

Which meant that when her phone rang, her
rebellious heart immediately hoped it was Nick.
When she saw it was her mother, disappointment
and pleasure sprang forth in equal measure. She
pressed the phone and set it on speaker mode.

"Hi, Mom!" she said. "Merry Christmas! I'm
building a gingerbread house right now."

"Merry Christmas, dear!" her mother said. "Is
it for Christmas dinner?"

"Yep, for Hettie Mae. It's the least I can do,"
Becca said.

"You back home after the nor'easter?"

"Yep, safe and sound."

"Well, that's good. I was worried all night.
How much snow fell? How bad was it?"

"We got a *lot*," Becca said with a chuckle. "I
have so much shoveling to do."

"Did Nick drive you home himself? Did you
call for a cab? How does it work up there in
Heartsprings Valley?"

"Oh, he drove me himself," Becca said, choosing to omit the mode of transportation. If her mother found out she'd hitched a ride on the back of a snowmobile in the middle of a blizzard, she'd never hear the end of it! "But before he drove me home, we made a pit stop of sorts."

"A pit stop? What do you mean?"

"A farmer with a pregnant llama needed Nick's help delivering the baby."

"A pregnant *what*?"

"A pregnant llama."

"And you went with him?"

"Yep."

"To a llama farm?"

"Yep."

"Well, my goodness."

"The farmers — a very nice couple named Marianne and Angus — even let me pitch in."

"What do you mean, pitch in?"

"I helped get the baby into a bath of warm water, and I helped with her first feeding."

She heard her mother say to someone, "Becca helped deliver a baby llama on a farm last night!" Then: "Bathed her and fed her." Then: "Your younger brother wants to know if it was gross."

Becca laughed. "A little bit, yes. Especially the afterbirth."

"Okay, enough of that," her mom said firmly, presumably in response to something inappropriate her brother had just said. "Not on Christmas Day." Then, returning her attention to Becca, she said, "We'll be sitting down to dinner around four. We'll all be thinking of you and wishing you were here."

"I know, Mom. I wish I could be there, too."

"What time is dinner at Hettie Mae's?"

"Around four, I think."

"Will you have enough time to finish up the gingerbread house?"

"Just barely," Becca said with a glance at her construction project. "If I'm lucky."

"What about your new friend, Nick?" her mom said. "What's he doing?"

What about Nick, indeed? "I'm not sure."

"Does he have family there? Is he spending Christmas with them?"

Becca sighed. She knew what her mom was really asking: Was Nick single? She knew her mom wasn't going to stop asking questions until she got the answer she was really after — she was very determined that way — so Becca decided to cut to the chase.

"He lost his wife in a car crash two years ago, so yes, I suppose he's single. And no, his family's not from here. I'm not sure what he's doing today. He's not really the Christmas type."

"Not the Christmas type? Nonsense," her

mom said. Then she added, "I'm sorry to hear about his wife."

"He told me he finds the Christmas season painful because it reminds him of his wife. So ... he's taking a break from it."

"Oh, I see," her mom said, then paused. "Well, everyone deals with loss in his or her own way, don't they. Like you, dear."

"Me?" Becca said, her heart suddenly thumping. *What was her mom hinting at?*

There was another pause as her mom gathered her thoughts. "I know why you had to be in Heartsprings Valley and not here for Christmas," she finally said, very gently. "I know how difficult the past two holiday seasons have been for you without Dave."

Becca found her way to a chair and sat down. *Her mother had known all along?* She felt herself begin to choke up. "I'm sorry, Mom. I just knew I needed...."

"Honey," her mom said. "I understand. In your own way, you needed a break as well."

The two of them allowed the silence to linger. Through the phone line, Becca heard the compassion and understanding in her mother's voice. The tears came then, as her guilt about lying to her mom, the uncertainty and anxiety about holding back the full truth from her, began to melt away. "I love you so much, Mom."

"I know, dear," her mom said. "I love you, too. All of us here do."

There was another pause, and then Becca heard the familiar voice of her smart-alecky younger brother Bobby filling the phone.

"Okay, you two," he said, "stop with the blubbering. Geesh!"

Becca laughed through her tears. "Oh, you."

"Merry Christmas, sis. What's this about you adopting a dog?"

Becca got up from her chair at the kitchen table and got herself a paper towel to dry her eyes and blow her nose. She didn't bother disguising the sounds of her nose-clearing, either, making sure the volume was loud enough to prompt Bobby to say —

"Gross, sis. That's just plain gross."

Becca laughed. "Merry Christmas, little bro. And yes, I adopted a dog. His name is Bowzer. You'll get to meet him when you visit."

"Good. We're all missing you. Of course, there is one benefit of you being up there: More of Mom's famous apple pie for me."

A pang of hunger tore through Becca's stomach. "Don't you dare rub that in, mister. I claim the right of revenge if you utter one more word about that pie!"

Bobby laughed. "Okay, in the spirit of the Christmas, I'll grant a one-day rubbing-in reprieve. Hope you have a great day up there, sis. Love you. Here's Mom."

"Love you, too. Merry Christmas!"

Her mom came back on. "Oh, you two. The ribbing will never cease, will it?"

"Never," Becca said with a smile. She glanced at the time and breathed in sharply. "Oh, gosh, I've got so much to do, and so little time."

"Then I'll let you get to it," her mom said. "Merry Christmas, dear. Love you!"

"Merry Christmas. Love you, too!"

CHAPTER 30

*I*t was amazing how much one was able to do when there was barely any time to get it done. In the space of a few frantic hours, Becca plowed through a hefty list of to-do items with a determination that surprised her. Gingerbread house-building and decorating were the main priority, of course — making sure the walls and roof were cemented into place, then whipping up even more icing, and of course taking out her trusty decorating toolkit — her stash of sugary, glittery sprinkles and specialty frostings — to apply the finishing touches.

In-between the decorating steps — a whirl-wind of activity! For the first time in her entire life, with gloved hands and aching shoulders, she picked up a snow shovel and cleared a path from her doorway to the sidewalk. She found herself enjoying the exercise initially, getting into a rhythm with the shovel, digging deep into the fresh show and tossing big shovelfuls to the side. But soon enough, pleasure turned to heavy breathing and sweating. By the time she finished, her cheeks were flushed with effort and her already-sore muscles were begging her to stop.

Still, despite the pain, she'd done it — cleared her first-ever path through the snow — and she felt proud about that. Okay, proud and sore. Okay, mostly sore, but at least the darned chore was done!

Hettie Mae called after lunch and told her to be ready at four. "Frank will swing by to pick up you and Bowzer," she told her.

"You don't need to have him do that," Becca said.

"He likes it," Hettie Mae said. "Don't you worry."

"Are you sure?"

"I wouldn't say it if I wasn't."

"Then thank you. And did you say Bowzer?"

"Of course. We can't let him stay home alone at Christmas."

Becca smiled. "Bowzer and I will see you at four."

Besides the shoveling and gingerbread-house decorating, her other main task was decorating herself. She showered and shampooed, then got herself dressed in an outfit she'd already picked out: a holiday sweater (soft white wool, with a festive red-and-green candy-cane pattern across the front), dark slacks, and sensible low-heeled black pumps. The pumps were a question mark given the weather, but she figured that as long as she was careful walking outside across the icy ground, she'd be fine. For makeup, she opted for the same low-stress approach she'd used the day before: light foundation and the same soft red lip balm, with a hint of eyeliner.

She checked her lobes for her silver reindeer earrings — still there, and still looking sparkly — then turned her attention to her hands. Her fingernails were fine, but just barely. She was overdue for a manicure — she made a mental note to get a recommendation from Hettie Mae. She also realized that, with her wedding band stored away, her fingers looked rather bare. Stepping into her bedroom, she opened her jewelry case and selected a red ruby ring set in a silver band. She'd worn the ring throughout her high school and college years. With a smile, she slipped it onto her right hand's third finger, enjoying not only its appearance, but how it reminded her of how she was back then, when the world felt big and new and wide-open.

The ruby ring made her feel ... *refreshed*, she realized. Satisfied, she closed the drawer and returned to the kitchen, where her gingerbread house was awaiting its final touches.

Bowzer ambled in and cocked his head, watching her as she bent down to apply a sprinkling of green glitter to the wreath she'd added to the house's front door.

"Just a few final touches," she said, glancing at the clock. "And just in time, too. Our ride will be here any minute."

She stood back and carefully examined her first Heartsprings Valley gingerbread house. Ideally, she would have preferred another couple hours to add the small but important details that mattered so much. Still, this house — simpler and more straightforward than her usual creations — pleased her. It looked a lot like her new home, with white frosting applied in horizontal bands, just like the white clapboard siding of her cottage. On the roof lay a thick layer of fresh white snow-icing, just like the nor'easter's bounty on her roof at that very moment. The front door was the same dark red, with a beautiful green wreath decorating it. For the windows, she'd chosen red window panes and light blue curtains. And for the all-important dashes of holiday green, she'd fashioned evergreen shrubbery along the front and sides of the house.

With the extra white icing, she'd built a snowman and set it in front of the house, creating eyes, a nose, and a smile with carefully selected sprinkles.

Her gingerbread house looked, in a word, delicious. Her stomach grumbled in agreement.

From outside, she heard a car approaching. She stepped into the living room and saw, through her front window, an SUV pull up. She watched Hettie Mae hop down from the passenger side and make her way down Becca's freshly shoveled path to the cottage's front steps.

Even before the first knock, Becca pulled open the door. "Welcome, Hettie Mae! Come on in. I wasn't expecting you to come out here, too."

"Thank you." Hettie Mae stamped her boots on the steps and walked in. Bowzer dashed up, tail wagging, and greeted her with a friendly sniff.

"Almost ready. Let me get my coat and Bowzer's leash and the gingerbread house and we'll be ready to go."

"Making progress with the unpacking, I see," Hettie Mae said, surveying the living room as Becca shrugged into her coat.

"It sure doesn't feel like it," Becca said with a laugh. "I still have so much to do."

"Is that a homemade quilt?" Hettie Mae asked, gesturing to the sofa. She stepped closer and ran a discerning eye over the quilt while Becca bent down to fasten Bowzer's leash to his collar.

"My Grandma Ellie made it for me when I was little. It's one of my favorite Christmas keepsakes."

"It's a beautiful piece. The stitching is exceptional. It really captures the spirit of the season. Now, what's this about a gingerbread house?"

"I made one. Just finished it, in fact."

"Becca," Hettie Mae protested, "you didn't have to do that."

"I wanted to," Becca insisted.

"That's very thoughtful of you."

With the leash attached to the dog, Becca gestured for Hettie Mae to follow her into the kitchen, where the freshly decorated gingerbread house stood on a plate on the dining table.

"Oh, it's beautiful," Hettie Mae said. "Looks just like this cottage."

"I felt inspired by it," Becca said, then held up the leash and added, "Would you mind taking Bowzer? I can carry the gingerbread out to the car."

"A good plan," Hettie Mae said. She took the leash from Becca and led Bowzer out the front door. On the steps, Becca eased past her and headed straight down the freshly cleared path to the SUV, where a man — Hettie's Mae's husband Frank — hopped out.

"Here, young lady," he said. "I'll hold that until you two get settled in."

"Thank you." Carefully, she passed the ginger-bread house into his waiting arms.

From the front porch, Hettie Mae said, "Becca, you and Bowzer hop into the back seat. You got everything you need?"

Becca checked her coat pocket for her phone and keys. "I'm good."

Hettie Mae firmly shut the front door and jiggled the handle to make sure if was locked, then followed Bowzer down the path. Bowzer eagerly sniffed Frank's leg and looked back and forth between the three humans, ready for what-ever fun might come next.

"Come on, Bowzer," Becca said. "Let's get in back." She took the leash from Hettie Mae, opened the car door, and encouraged Bowzer to jump in. A bit awkwardly, the big guy clambered in, and Becca followed.

Hettie Mae made her way around to the passenger side, then got in and buckled up.

Frank gently placed the gingerbread house on his wife's lap, shut the door, then stepped around to his seat and got in.

Before turning on the engine, he swung around.

"I'm Frank, by the way," he said to Becca, a friendly, good-humored grin. "Hettie Mae's plus-one." Dressed in boots, jeans and red sweater, he looked like a solid, dependable kind of guy, his movements deliberate and careful. He had a reddened, weathered face, framed by a short-cropped silver-grey beard.

"Very nice to meet you, Frank. Thank you so much for the door-to-door service."

"Happy to. Nice to get out of the house every now and then and stretch my legs."

"Are you okay with the gingerbread, Hettie Mae?" Becca asked. "I can take it, if you'd like."

"Nonsense," Hettie Mae replied. "You and Bowzer just sit back and relax."

The SUV pulled away from the curb and headed down Pine Street toward the center of town. The freshly cleared streets were surrounded on all sides by the storm's hefty snowfall. Every roof, every tree, every inch of ground seemed to groan under the weight. The late-afternoon sun cast a pale light over the homes and holiday decorations — snowmen, reindeer, trees wrapped in lights — that seemed to be everywhere.

"By the way, a change in plans," Hettie Mae said. "I got a call from Dr. Gail, and she invited us to join her at the vet clinic for the potluck."

CHAPTER 31

hey were going to the potluck instead? Becca blinked with surprise, but immediately recovered when she realized, with a flush of pleasure, that she'd be able to see Dr. Gail and show her how well she and Bowzer were doing.

"It's so nice of her to include us," Becca said, pleased.

"We made way too much food for just three people, so why not share. Plus, you'll get a chance to meet more of your new neighbors."

"Sounds great."

A minute later, the Victorian spires of the vet clinic came into view. A number of cars were already parked in the driveway and along the street in front of the building.

"A nice crowd's already there," Frank said. He found a spot on the street about half a block from the clinic and got the SUV parked.

"Hettie Mae, you take the gingerbread house in, and Becca and I will grab the rest."

With a nod, Hettie Mae pushed open her door and stepped out. Carefully, with the gingerbread house balanced in her arms, she made her way toward the clinic.

"Okay, Bowzer," Becca said, firmly holding onto his leash, "let's go see your pals." She and Bowzer scooted out of the SUV and joined Frank at the back of the SUV.

Frank picked up a bag filled with covered dishes. "You okay with this one?"

"Sure, no problem," Becca said, taking hold of the bag, which was heavy but manageable. "Need me to carry anything else?"

"I got the rest. You go on inside."

Cautiously, Becca made her way down the sidewalk toward the clinic, leash in one hand, bag in the other. The air was sharp and crisp and fresh, with a hint of pine. The sidewalk was cleared and salted, but even so, she paid close attention to her steps, anxious about slipping.

Next to her, Bowzer had figured out where they were going and was starting to tug excitedly on his leash.

"Slow down, boy. We'll be there soon enough."

As she approached the steps leading up to the front door, she saw through the windows that folks were already gathered inside. Murmurs of conversation and laughter spilled from the house as the front door swung open to reveal —

Abby from the chocolate shop!

"Abby!" Becca said, delighted.

"Merry Christmas, Becca!" Abby said.

Becca made her way up the steps, set down the bag, and gave Abby a friendly hug, then stepped back to admire the Santa Claus clasp pinned to her friend's red sweater. "That pin is so perfect."

"Thank you."

Bowzer bumped her knee to greet her, causing Abby to laugh and reach down to give him a pat. "Hello, Bowzer, how are you today?"

Wagging his tail, Bowzer gazed up at Abby affectionately.

"I think he's happy to be here," Becca said.

"I'm sure he's excited about being able to see all his pals," Abby replied. She picked up the bag of food. "Let's get you inside."

They scooted in, and Abby helped Becca take off her heavy winter coat and hang it up it up on a coat rack near the front door.

A woman approached and said, "If you'd like, I can take Bowzer downstairs to see his pals."

"Are you sure?" Becca said.

"Happy to," the woman said. "I volunteer here, and I miss this guy!" She reached down and gave Bowzer a friendly pat. "And I know he'll be happy to see his friends."

"Thank you so much." She knelt down and gave Bowzer a hug. "You be a good boy, okay? I'll come down for you later."

Bowzer gave her an affectionate bark and nuzzled her cheek. He was such an adorable dog. In just two days, he'd brought such joy to her life.

As she stood back up and watched the volunteer lead Bowzer toward his friends downstairs in the kennel, Abby turned to Becca. "That dog is so special."

"He sure is," Becca said. "He's the best."

Abby peeked into the bag full of food. "Oh my, you brought a lot!"

"Not me. This is all Hettie Mae." She picked up the bag and stepped with Abby into the big spacious waiting room. Together, they navigated their way through the crowd to the long table laden with potluck dishes of all sorts.

Hettie Mae was already there, setting the gingerbread house between two plates of Christmas cookies. She turned around and said, "I'll take the bag and get everything out."

"Here you go," Becca said, setting it carefully on the table.

Abby's gaze fell on the gingerbread house. "Oh, Hettie Mae, will you look at that."

"No thanks to me," Hettie Mae said as she starting unpacking the bag and setting food containers on the table. "This delightful cookie cottage is Becca's."

Abby turned toward Becca. "You did this?"

Becca blushed. "Guilty as charged."

"It's beautiful," Abby said. A gleam came to her eye. "I'm envisioning a gingerbread house in my shop window. In a place of honor. Surrounded by chocolates, of course. A gingerbread house made by the town's new librarian."

Becca's eyes widened with surprise. "Really?"

Abby nodded. "You have a gift for capturing the spirit of Christmas."

For the second time that day, tears threatened. But tears would not do — not now! — so Becca blinked rapidly, willing them away. "I'd be honored to make a gingerbread house for your store window. In fact, once I have a bit more time, I'd like to make a gingerbread house based on this big old Victorian house."

"That would be wonderful," Abby said. "But based on this place? That's so ambitious. There are so many angles and spires, and turrets and —"

"I know," she said with a laugh. "I'm probably crazy. But the vet clinic has already made such an impact in my life. I'd like to give it a shot."

She felt an arm on her shoulder and turned around to find Dr. Gail smiling at her.

"What did I just overhear? Something about turrets and spires?"

Abby jumped in. "Becca's going to make a gingerbread replica of the vet clinic to display in my shop window."

"That sounds wonderful," Dr. Gail said. Her eyes fell on Becca's gingerbread cottage on the table. "Did you make that? It's lovely."

"Thank you," Becca said. "And thank you for hosting us this afternoon. What a nice crowd."

"It's so important to spend time with friends and loved ones at Christmas," Dr. Gail said. "I was just downstairs in the kennel and can report that Bowzer is happily playing with his pals."

At that moment, Hettie Mae stepped up between Abby and Dr. Gail and whispered something in their ears. The three women swung toward the front door.

Becca's gaze followed. A man had just arrived. He was taking off his mackinaw, his back toward them as he hung the coat on the rack near the door. He was wearing a button-down white collared shirt tucked into jeans. He took off a ski cap, revealing a head of shaggy brown hair that could use a bit of straightening up.

She'd known who the new arrival was the instant she saw him, but she still felt a rush of mounting anticipation as he turned around and she caught the handsome profile of his face and confirmed that it was —

Nick!

CHAPTER 32

*S*he watched him step into the main room, his eyes wandering over the crowd. When he found Dr. Gail, he made his way toward her, a smile on his face.

It was only after he'd given Dr. Gail a quick hug that he saw Becca. He blinked, his mouth dropping open.

At the exact same time, both he and Becca said:

"What are you doing here?"

"I —" they both said at the same time, then stopped as the same thought simultaneously occurred to them.

In unison, they turned toward the trio of women — Abby, Hettie Mae, and Dr. Gail — who were now standing together, arms linked, staring at them with big satisfied smiles on their faces.

Aha! Becca thought. *So that's what's going on.* Abby and Gail and Hettie Mae had joined forces and conspired together. They'd arranged for this surprise to occur! Part of her wanted to protest about this secret plan to get Nick and her into the same room. But the bigger part of her — the much bigger part of her, she knew — was touched and grateful.

Nick stared at the three women with narrowed eyes. Then he chuckled and shook his head. "We've been set up," he said to Becca, sounding half-annoyed and half-admiring. "By a trio of born meddlers."

"Total meddlers," Becca agreed, a big smile on her face.

Abby laughed, and Hettie Mae said, "You're looking quite nice today, Nick."

Nick smiled at the three women, then turned his attention back to Becca, a hint of playfulness in his dark brown eyes.

"Still happy you decided to move here?" he asked her. "These women are relentless, you know. Once they set their mind on something, watch out. They're ferocious. Unstoppable."

Becca laughed, and threw her new friends a grateful glance. "I'm beginning to figure that out." A warm feeling came at seeing how affectionately Nick was talking about the three women. She liked seeing him in an upbeat mood — liked seeing how happiness transformed his handsome face.

At that moment, Hettie Mae took Abby and Dr. Gail's by their arms and said, "Ladies, I need help with something on the other side of the room."

Dr. Gail smiled, and Abby said, "Merry Christmas, Dr. Nick."

"Merry Christmas, ladies," Nick said.

He and Becca watched the trio step to the other side of the room, where they busily pretended to not pay attention to them.

Nick couldn't help but grin. "What excuse did Hettie Mae give you to get you here?"

"She said she made too much food for three people," Becca said. "Which I'm sure is true."

"Very conveniently true," he agreed.

She was about to reply but found herself pausing, unsure how to ask what she wanted to ask.

Be strong, she told herself.

"And you? Why are you here? I thought you'd quit Christmas."

He went still as he absorbed her question, his expression growing serious. He'd shaved this morning, she saw — yesterday's stubble was long gone. Aside from his still-too-shaggy hair, he looked like he'd cleaned up and dressed for the occasion. He stepped closer, then reached out and took her hands in his. She nearly gasped as the same jolt as the day before raced through her.

"I realized something important last night, thanks to you."

"What's that?" she said, her tone much calmer than how she felt inside.

He cleared his throat, then said, his voice husky, "I'm ready to let Christmas back into my life."

"Oh," she said. Without warning, the room around them seemed to fade away. The sounds of crowd became indistinct. The air became very hot. She felt her cheeks flush pink.

He frowned, as if realizing something for the first time, and raised her left hand up to look at it.

"Your wedding ring," he said, the question lingering in his eyes.

She swallowed and, holding his gaze, willed her voice to remain steady. "It's in my dresser drawer, which is where it belongs, as a treasured memento of times past."

His deep brown eyes flashed with barely suppressed excitement. Without a word, her hand in his, he led her out of the room, away from the crowd, to the relative privacy of the front porch.

He shut the big front door, then reached

around her and pulled her toward him. She leaned in as his strong arms circled her waist. It was cold out here, the early evening air sharp and frigid, the Christmas lights on the porch rail offering only the faintest glow of illumination — but she didn't care about any of that right now.

She found herself aware again of how tall he was, how strong, how reassuring and comforting and, yes, so much more.

With a shy grin she couldn't control, she gazed up at him, her heart leaping when she saw he was looking back at her with tenderness and joy.

"I'm ready for Christmas again," he said. "And ready for love."

A lump pushed its way into her throat, her eyes springing fresh tears, as his right hand caressed her cheek.

"I'm ready for love, too," she said softly.

"I've wanted to do this since the moment we met," he said.

She inhaled his scent — hints of cologne and musk and soap, wonderfully mixed — as he leaned in, his lips brushing hers.

"Merry Christmas, Becca Jameson," he whispered.

"Merry Christmas, Nick Shepherd," she whispered back.

And then they kissed, their lips merging into one — two lost souls, through the miracle of the season, finding a new home.

THE END

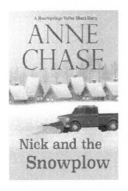

**A heartwarming holiday story about a
handsome veterinarian and the shy, beautiful
librarian he meets on Christmas Eve....**

Nick and the Snowplow is a companion to *Christmas
to the Rescue!*, the first novel in the Heartsprings
Valley Sweet Romance series. In *Christmas to the
Rescue!*, a young librarian named Becca gets

caught in a blizzard on Christmas Eve, finds shelter with a handsome veterinarian named Nick, and ends up experiencing the most surprising, adventure-filled night of her life.

Nick and the Snowplow, told from Nick's point of view, shows what happens after Nick brings Becca home at the end of their whirlwind evening.

This story is available FOR FREE when you sign up for Anne Chase's email newsletter.

Go to AnneChase.com to sign up and get your free story!

CHRISTMAS TO THE RESCUE!

A HEARTSPRINGS VALLEY SWEET
ROMANCE (BOOK 1)

'Twas the blizzard before Christmas...

Becca Jameson is a recent arrival in
Heartsprings Valley, ready for a fresh start in
life as the town's new librarian, three years
after the death of her beloved husband.

When a canine charmer named Bowzer
captures her heart at an "Adopt-a-Pet" event,
little does Becca realize that her furry pal will
drag her into the Christmas adventure of a
lifetime, complete with a fierce blizzard, a
pregnant llama, and a very handsome
veterinarian.

With holiday mayhem thrust upon her, Becca must navigate a storm of snowflakes and hot cocoa to rediscover the romance of Christmas -- and embrace a future filled with life and hope.

The Heartsprings Valley Sweet Romance series celebrates love during the most wonderful time of the year.

Christmas to the Rescue! (Book 1)

A Very Cookie Christmas (Book 2)

Sweet Apple Christmas (Book 3)

I Dream of Christmas (Book 4)

Available on Amazon!

A VERY COOKIE CHRISTMAS

A HEARTSPRINGS VALLEY SWEET
ROMANCE (BOOK 2)

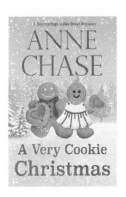

Her craziest Christmas — ever!

Clara is a super-organized and overworked
New York publicity assistant, eager for a
relaxing Christmas break with her beloved dad
in her hometown of Heartsprings Valley.

Just as she's heading home, her boss delivers
shocking news:

Their biggest client, a demanding Broadway
star named Melody, has decided to visit
Heartsprings Valley!

Oh, my!

More complications pile on, one after another, culminating in Clara's surprise encounter with Luke, her high-school crush.

The two of them haven't seen each other in a decade, they're both grown up now, and Luke's interest in her is immediately clear.

What's a girl to do?

With holiday insanity threatening to drive her crazy, Clara must listen to what her heart is quietly whispering about life and love —

And about where she truly belongs.

The Heartsprings Valley Sweet Romance series celebrates love during the most wonderful time of the year.

Christmas to the Rescue! (Book 1)

A Very Cookie Christmas (Book 2)

Sweet Apple Christmas (Book 3)

I Dream of Christmas (Book 4)

Available now!

SWEET APPLE CHRISTMAS

A HEARTSPRINGS VALLEY SWEET
ROMANCE (BOOK 3)

A recipe for Christmas romance!

When Holly, a hardworking cafe owner, meets
a handsome orchard farmer named Gabriel,
their connection is immediate.

As these two busy people get to know each
other, Holly finds herself torn between the
emotional importance of "keeping it real" and
her heart's stubborn desire to give love a
chance.

When a surprise from the past threatens her
dreams, can Holly dig deep to embrace a
future filled with hope and happiness?

The Heartsprings Valley Sweet Romance series celebrates love during the most wonderful time of the year.

Christmas to the Rescue! (Book 1)

A Very Cookie Christmas (Book 2)

Sweet Apple Christmas (Book 3)

I Dream of Christmas (Book 4)

Available now!

I DREAM OF CHRISTMAS

A HEARTSPRINGS VALLEY SWEET
ROMANCE (BOOK 4)

Stuck in a storm … with a handsome stranger!

Melody Connelly, the Broadway singing star
with a heart of gold, is back with a romance of
her own!

Two years after first visiting Heartsprings
Valley, Melody has bought and restored a
grand Victorian home just outside of town.

As the holiday draws near, she's busy getting
her new home ready to host her mom for the
best Christmas ever.

But when a winter storm hits, Melody finds

herself snowbound with James, a handsome furniture craftsman.

Surprised by their unexpected connection, Melody believes the universe is nudging her toward romance — until a blast from the past throws everything into doubt.

Now Melody must ask: Does her dream of a perfect Christmas include a chance at romance?

And if so, with whom?

The Heartsprings Valley Sweet Romance series celebrates love during the most wonderful time of the year.

Christmas to the Rescue! (Book 1)

A Very Cookie Christmas (Book 2)

Sweet Apple Christmas (Book 3)

I Dream of Christmas (Book 4)

Available soon!

ABOUT THE AUTHOR

Spoiler alert: I love Christmas! The Heartsprings Valley Sweet Romance series celebrates the joy and warmth of the holiday season. I hope you enjoy reading these stories as much as I love writing them.

Though I live now in the bustling Bay Area, far from the small town I grew up in (population: 2,000), I remember my childhood days — and my family's wonderful Christmas traditions — with fondness and gratitude.

My email newsletter is a great way to find out about new books and gain access to exclusive content. Plus, did I mention all the delicious recipes? :-)

Go to **AnneChase.com** to sign up.

Thank you, and Merry Christmas!

Made in the USA
Coppell, TX
15 June 2022